**Featu**
**Paranoi**

# The Spirits At Jim's Bar

*To Margaret,
All the best,
Dean*

## Dean Fraser

Published 2023

2023 Copyright ©

The author has asserted their right under the Copyright, Designs and Patents Act 1988 to be identified as the author of the book and work.

All rights reserved. No part of the publication may be reproduced, stored in a retrieval system or transmitted in any form or by any means, electronic, photocopying, recording or otherwise, without the prior permission of the copyright owner. Although the author and publisher have made every effort to ensure that the information in this book was correct at press time, the author and publisher do not assume and thereby disclaim any liability to any party for any loss, damage, or disruption caused by errors or omissions, whether such errors or omissions result from negligence, accident, or any other cause. This book is not intended as a substitute for the medical advice of medical professionals. The reader should regularly consult a chosen medical professional in matters relating to their health and particularly with respect to any symptoms that may require diagnosis or medical attention.

ISBN: 9798853354890

## CHAPTER

PAGE NUMBER

| | | |
|---|---|---|
| 1. | THE SPIRITS AT JIM'S BAR | 004 |
| 2. | SUICIDE CAR PARK | 030 |
| 3. | POLTERGEIST IN STORAGE | 042 |
| 4. | DEPOSITED AT THE BANK | 052 |
| 5. | DEMON HUNTING AFTER MIDNIGHT | 062 |
| 6. | THIS TIME IT'S PERSONAL | 088 |
| 7. | THE HAUNTED APARTMENT | 108 |
| 8. | ROMAN INVASION | 122 |
| 9. | COULD FLORENCE BE HEALED? | 132 |
| 10. | A NOT SO EMPTY FACTORY | 142 |
| 11. | THE COUNT AND HIS CASTLE | 148 |
| 12. | BERTIE MACDONALD | 170 |
| 13. | THE COUNTESS MARY KNEW SHE WAS DEAD | 186 |
| 14. | MURDER IN THE WINE CELLAR | 202 |
| 15. | DOWN IN THE DUNGEON | 224 |
| 16. | WE BOUGHT THE FARM | 260 |
| 17. | AUTHOR'S NOTE | 270 |
| 18. | ABOUT THE AUTHOR | 272 |

# 1

# THE SPIRITS AT JIM'S BAR

"Under absolutely no circumstances go anywhere near my ghosts with anything approaching an exorcism!"

Ghosts meant plenty of free publicity through the media and more importantly a bar full of customers; the last thing the owner needed was them gone!

This case would turn out to be far more complex than I first imagined, but more of that later, for now I needed to go through the formalities of taking on the investigation and here was a story in itself.

The email arrived in my inbox one afternoon in the height of summer. I'd been sat there contemplating the idea of taking myself off for a walk along the busy seafront of my chosen home town of Folkestone when my laptop pinged announcing someone in cyberspace had decided that out of the seven billion of us sharing this blue-green ball in space, I was the chosen one to be contacted.

The email came from the owner of Jim's Bar. I'd never heard of the place, but then I'm not one for pubs, so it's no surprise it wasn't on my radar. Jim's Bar happened to be located in Dover, the next town up the coast from me in Kent. "Dear Mr Darke, I wish to offer you a lockdown at my bar and I shall pay you well for your time". This was all the email said, without giving away any clues as to why I ended up as the recipient of such a kind offer. Okay, so I admit I do get a lot of emails from people wanting my services and they usually tell all straight away about why they need my particular kind of expertise.

I emailed back "A lockdown at a bar traditionally means an invitation for a little illicit after-hours drinking; if that's not what you're offering, what had you got in mind?" The reply came back almost immediately and I don't mind admitting caught my attention "Ghosts Mr Darke; positively oodles of lovely ghosts!" I was hooked.

I emailed over my phone number and asked for a call the following morning to arrange a suitable time to meet and discuss things further. This call came through mid-morning and the owner of Jim's asked me to please drop in for a meeting as soon as was convenient. Dover is only a short distance from me; I set-off immediately, taking the train instead of dealing with the chaos of trying to park my old van in Dover at the height of summer. Within an hour of our conversation I arrived to meet the owner of Jim's Bar. I hadn't been inside the place before, I'm repelled by the stench of stale beer and alcohol induced false merriment; like I said, pubs and clubs are not really my scene.

Owner 'Jim' wasn't actually called Jim, but was a youngish woman it would be difficult not to notice named Robyn Humphries.

By now the bar was filling-up with their early lunchtime customers; Robyn suggested we adjourn to her office to continue our conversation. I observed her from behind as I followed her along the corridor to her office; it wasn't an unpleasant task. She wasn't too far off my height and I'm above averagely tall for a man. I estimated Robyn to be at the maximum thirty years old and probably less; she wore a below knee-length black leather skirt and buccaneer boots, an oversized white shirt, a vintage blue military style jacket draped over her shoulders and her long chestnut hair was tied in a thick side-braid hanging down past her left breast. Robyn was more beautiful than any pirate I'd ever seen in some movie; she looked like she'd left her pirate's sloop moored down in Dover Harbour and then headed along to our meeting. Robyn smelled pleasantly of a heady fragrance I couldn't quite identify.

I didn't bother asking why she chose Jim's for the name of her bar, this was likely something she got asked all the time and probably got bored of answering; in no way relevant to my possible case, this didn't seem too important; I prefer to keep my attention fixed on what I need know.

Once we were seated in her office the conversation flowed easily between us. Robyn was well-spoken without a trace of any accent "Can I firstly tell you Mr Darke I know well of your reputation as I avidly watch all your lockdown videos; I am beyond excited to think you might possibly accept my offer to investigate my bar" I smiled at Robyn, which I found made her smile back at me, guess I would be smiling a lot at her then; I answered "Thank you for that Robyn, I am sure I would find your case compelling. In your email you mentioned positively oodles of lovely ghosts" Robyn exclaimed "Mr Darke, you are in for such a paranormal treat here! We believe there are at least three ghosts frequenting Jim's Bar, and expert that you are, you may well find even more!" Robyn continued "To fill you in on the history Mr Darke, this is an old building and it's been a public house for at least three hundred years; in the 19th century it also served as the local assizes or court; our cellars were once used as the holding cells for prisoners awaiting trial, there is a particularly nasty ghost down there!"

At this revelation I looked across at Robyn, and asked "How is it nasty?" Robyn replied "Weird stuff occurs down in the cellars Mr Darke. I don't wish to share too much. I would prefer to see what happens when you come along for a lockdown". I pondered for a moment and then added "It's Darke, no need for the Mr. My parents were Pagan hippies living life by their own rules. They decided Om would make a great first name for me. The legacy of my childhood left me a Pagan Wiccan with a tendency towards Buddhism!" Robyn's eyes went wide and she looked at me knowingly, I liked her looking at me knowingly, I said "I usually go by just Darke""

Robyn smiled warmly over at me, only extremely melting my heart in the process "I am going to call you Om; I hope you are okay with that?" I smiled back and nodded my head in the affirmative. She could easily have proclaimed she would call me Lulu-Belle and I would have nodded to agree, just to see her smile at me again in that way. Robyn continued "We've got glasses jumping from off the shelf behind the bar, a shadow figure on the stairs leading down to the cellars we think we caught on CCTV, I shall show you that before you go and as I mentioned lots of weird stuff happens down in the cellars. We have customers frequently getting touched on the arm. When we are closed and all is quiet in the bar, we hear conversations just beyond the edge of our hearing. It sounds as if some people are talking behind a wall. Oh, I almost forgot to mention there's a certain seat cushion in our function room upstairs, I shall also show you this in a minute, which goes down as if someone is sat there. You want ghosts Om, take your pick!"

I asked the obvious question; I thought to I ought to at some point "What exactly is it you want me to do here Robyn? Do you want me to exorcise these ghosts for you?"

"Under absolutely no circumstances go anywhere near my ghosts with anything approaching an exorcism, Om!" Robyn laughed as she said this but was clearly serious; she continued "Ghosts keep my customers coming through the door to see if they might get some paranormal experience; I only want to know as much as you can tell me about my ghosts please Om and that's all!" She added "I shall pay you £200 per hour for your time" Robyn leant back in her chair "Will demonologist Anna be consulting with you again on this case? I believe she shall enjoy herself down in our cellar" I replied "Anna and I worked together for a while, now we don't, such is the way of life" Robyn didn't look devastated at this news.

Anna and I had been partners, and I mean in every sense, for something over two years. We met when I got called in to investigate this old office building in London and Anna was the member of staff designated to show me around. It turned out she was quite the expert on demons. We'd kind of clicked straight away and soon grew close. At this time we were having, as Anna had described it "Some space to ourselves Darke, I'm going to stay with my mum in Prague for six months, if we both still want to be together after this I'll come back to you". Anna was a free spirit and adrenalin junkie; some of her actions during our cases frankly scared me; the woman enjoyed provoking demonic entities! More than a fair share of this recklessness spilled over into our home life. Anna was convinced the break was just what we needed; I got no say in the matter. I wasn't holding my breath waiting for her possible return one fine day from her home country of the Czech Republic or Czechia as we must now call it. The country was known as Czechoslovakia when Anna was born. Prague is one of my favourite cities; I held no plans to visit there at any point in the foreseeable future.

Back in Dover I voiced the next obvious question "Robyn, if your bar is open from mid-morning through until late at night, how am I going to properly investigate?" I continued "I would need the building to myself, Robyn."

"I thought it might be like that and this is not a problem Om; agree to do the investigation next Monday evening and for you I shall close the bar! Seriously, this investigation of yours means so much to me you shall have the place to yourself for as long as you require from 6pm onwards. And do please take all the time you require to thoroughly investigate Jim's!"

"Okay that sounds perfect Robyn; I agree I will be here on Monday arriving shortly before 6pm" Robyn responded "Fantastic Om! I cannot wait to see what you discover here at Jim's!"

I'd already told Robyn I would take all the filming collected on the evening to analyse for any spirits my cameras may have captured, and then edit it all into a video that made sense. Robyn asked if it might be possible for an exclusive premier before it went live on my video channel. I agreed I would meet again with Robyn after a week to play her the video before I posted it up online. I was already counting down the hours.

PLANNING

I don't usually do too much of this. Not my thing.

If this investigation was going to achieve anything, this time some planning beforehand was essential.

There were three locations Robyn wanted me to investigate:

1. The cellars complete with their bad energy.

2. The upstairs function room, once the court and where this cushion on a certain chair allegedly goes down as if occupied by an unseen person.
3. Finally the main bar, where glasses apparently fly off shelves and customers get touched on the arm.

I resolved to investigate Jim's Bar in the above order. This would be my first solo investigation since Anna left. On the one hand it would feel strange not having her back and Anna having mine. On the other hand this is how I started out as a paranormal investigator, with just myself to think about. Once more returning to the danger and rawness of some of my earlier investigations admittedly got my juices flowing which found me looking forward to this lockdown; and not just because of Robyn Humphries, although I admit the woman had some magic about her that had caught my full attention!

ARRIVAL AT JIM'S BAR

Jim's Bar was deserted; no staff or any thirsty customers waiting to be served. Robyn stood there looking ravishing in her pirate gear awaiting my arrival. She enthusiastically greeted me when I walked through the door with 'CLOSED' written largely upon it; she shook my hand and then stood up on her toes to kiss my cheek, I didn't fight her off. She smelled exquisite up close. She said "Om, I am too excited to have you on a lockdown at my bar! All quiet as promised. Look, why don't you put all your stuff in my office and take your time to get set-up? Do you need me to switch off all the lights before I leave you to it?"

I replied "Thank you Robyn, I'll use your office as my base of operations, if that's okay?" Robyn smiled warmly at me in the affirmative and my heart melted just a little more, I said "No thanks Robyn, I don't need the lights turned off all the time; I'm not making a television paranormal show here to add some extra drama and anyway likely I'd only end up tripping over all your chairs and tables as I am stumbling around unable to see!" Robyn laughed at this. Her soft gentle laugh sounded like a gift from the goddess to me personally.

I had one request to make "Robyn, is it possible for you to switch off your CCTV for the duration of my lockdown? The electromagnetic energy it emits could interfere with some of my equipment". Okay, between you and me this wasn't strictly true. The reality is, as impressed as I was with her empire that I was about to investigate and even more with the woman herself, I didn't really know Robyn and I didn't want her possibly overtly recording my every move to use later for free publicity. I'd firmly decided on the journey over I'd call-off my investigation if she hadn't agreed to me being CCTV free. With Robyn stood rightthere in front of me I knew there was no way I could have followed through with that decision and left; still it did feel kind of good when I thought it, like I was the one in control. Poor deluded male, of course women are the ones in charge and any guy accepting this, is in for one happier journey through life. I naturally did also intend turning off some of the lights at various points during the evening, but wanted the freedom to control this, as and when I chose.

"I can Om, I understand, for insurance purposes I shall just leave the outside cameras on, everything inside is now placed on standby until you are all done" Robyn added "By the way, when you were here the other day I noticed you asked for Bordeaux when I offered you a drink; I have left an uncorked bottle of a particularly nice vintage on the bar, with glasses for you to help yourself"

Although I don't drink alcohol when on cases this was still so thoughtful of Robyn. I thanked her and asked how long I would have for my lockdown. "Like I said the first time we met, please feel free to take as long as you need. I shall be waiting at home in Deal to hear from you, please bear with me Om when you text you are finished it is going to take me a tad of time to get back here to let you out!" I replied "I travelled here by train, then summer parking in Dover wouldn't be any issue, the last train back to Folkestone is at 11.10pm, but I plan on being all finished long before then Robyn!"

Robyn said "Have fun at Jim's and enjoy meeting all of my ghosts!" she stood up on her toes again to kiss my cheek. Now I am hardly some adolescent kid falling for a pretty face; Robyn though was the complete package, the total real deal; with her that close by me it took every last gram of my self-control to resist the temptation to properly kiss her back. With a smiling wave goodbye, Robyn locked the doors to leave me to my lockdown.

Robyn's exquisite perfume lingered in the air after she was gone. As I got myself prepared for my investigation I found her office heady with 'Fragrance of Robyn' as well. I did my level best to put the most alluring and magical woman to cross my path for years out of my mind to focus on what I was there for, she still kind of lingered in there, but I got on with my job of meeting her ghosts.

## LOCKDOWN AT JIM'S BAR

I said into my camera "Greetings! I am Cm Darke, here in the bustling port town of Dover in Kent for an evening lockdown at Jim's Bar. Owner Robyn Humphries called me in; she says there are multiple spirits here and not just the ones for sale to her customers! There are rumoured to be at least three ghosts that frequent Jim's Bar. I'll do my best to find out all I can about these spirits for Robyn. Anna Kostrová, resident demonologist, is taking a long vacation for some well-earned down-time, for this investigation I'll be working solo, just like in the old days."

I continued "I have three diverse locations to investigate at Jim's. First off I am going to be starting in the cellars; earlier off-camera I went for a walk through of the entire labyrinth of these cellars here at Jim's to familiarise myself with them. My first impressions are there is something that feels so wrong down there, but I'll no doubt find out more during my lockdown. Next, I am going to investigate the upstairs function room. Two hundred years ago this very same room was the local court; I want to see if the defendants in the court cases are still on trial in this very room. I'll explain all as I investigate. My final lockdown is here in this main bar where I am now standing. Many have witnessed weird stuff happening. I am going to be turning-off all the lights in here and try to psychically make contact with whatever it is haunting this bar. Let's go and investigate THE SPIRIT'S AT JIM'S BAR!"


THE CELLARS

"I am down here in the cellars at Jim's Bar for part one of my lockdown. These are extensive as you will see; the room I am presently in is filled with modern and noisy equipment used to pump beer, along with all those barrels over there" I panned my camera across the room "The strong aroma from all this beer is overwhelming, I need to move on from this room or I'll soon be getting 'very merry christmas' from just the smell!"

I slowly made my way out into a dark corridor "I've got all the lights turned out; what you can see on film is from my camera set on night vision. I am following my instinct here, I can't see too much but that's good because my senses are now more finely tuned to pick up on spirits or any demonic presences. I feel I should walk into this room to my right"

The room in question once formed part of the holding cell complex for the courts. "Oh this is fantastic! I am feeling a male spirit in this room. I'll turn on my digital recorder to see if I can get any EVPs. I'll ask him some questions and see if he wants to talk with me" I made myself comfortable sat on a wooden chair in this room and called out to the spirit "Hello I am called Om Darke, what is your name Sir?" to my camera I added "I can see on my recorder if I am getting any responses and nothing so far, but I'll leave it on this shelf recording while I am in here. I'll tell you what I am picking-up from this spirit; he's a young man, of this I am sure. He feels sad, but then he's here in a cell awaiting trial so maybe this is not too surprising! He passed-away young. He might not be aware of me"

After a few minutes the digital recorder lit up "Oh here we go!" picking it up I said "I'll play this back then you hear whatever I've caught along with me for the first time" I pressed play and "Girl?" could faintly be heard as if he was saying the word as a question "Thank you for that! No Sir, I am not a girl if that's a question you're asking me? I am definitely male!" I couldn't help but laugh, more seriously I said "Who are you Sir? Can you see me?" I waited, watching for any reply "Him!" came back.

I looked into my camera "Although it might appear like this spirit responded to me in this cell and my questions, I am not convinced. I honestly don't think he's aware of me and these are maybe just random words he's saying. Time to move onto another room"

I gingerly made my way along to the area I always intended would form the central focus of my cellar investigation that evening. "I am not too sure exactly what this room I am now entering was used for back in the day. Look at this full length recess in the wall over there like a cupboard without any door; and the floor is just dirt, unlike every other paved room in the cellar. During my earlier walk-through I got this feeling of unease" I looked directly into my camera "I felt an unpleasant presence in this room which pulled me back to know more!"

I intended to get to the bottom of whatever the room got used for; and discover more about the spirit that felt almost demonic; Anna would have been able to tell me for sure if it was.

"I am feeling an incredibly oppressive energy in this room, without any doubt something unpleasant went on in here" I continued "This spirit is aware of me, I know this for sure because he's stood right behind me! This is too weird. I am going to call this spirit out".

I spoke as steadily as I could "Hello, My name is Om Darke. I mean you no harm. I only seek to know your story!"

Nothing came back on my digital recorder. I felt in genuine danger. I swear I could hear Anna's voice in my head saying "You need to leave this room Darke! You can be harmed in here. This isn't a demon but one evil and nasty human. Darke, you need to leave right now!"

I know when to listen to my intuition and this was one time I needed to do precisely that. I promptly left the cellars with too many unanswered questions. Would my next lockdown in the function room be able to provide any answers?

## THE FUNCTION ROOM

"I am on the first floor in Jim's Bar in the function room; the sign on the door says it's called The Buccaneer Suite. This whole building is seriously old; as well as being a pub this once acted as the legal court for trying people for crimes. Where I investigated two floors below me in the cellars were the cells for holding prisoners. This very room I am now standing in was the court itself. I've got my digital recorder and shortly I'll see if any spirits want to talk with me. First, before I turn off all the lights, I want to show you a chair over here. Robyn tells me the cushion on this chair goes down as if someone invisible is sat in it, a spirit!"

I focussed close-up on chair in question "I am putting a motion detecting camera there on this table; if the cushion moves at all my camera sees and starts filming!"

I turned off the lights. As this case took place in the height of summer, and it was only 7.40pm, some shafts of daylight found its way into the room through tiny gaps in the wooden shutters covering the windows illuminating the dust particles hanging in the air.

Stood in the middle of the room I took a few moments to assess my surroundings and decide what to do. I spoke into my camera "I've placed my camera on the bar while I talk to you; this room for sure has an atmosphere once the lights go out! In daylight it feels welcoming, and yet now I sense the past all around me, like all the modern things are gone and I am right back in the old court. I am going to turn on my device and see if I can capture any EVPs".

"Is there anyone here who wants to communicate with me? Please talk to me, I mean you no harm" as usual I paused for a few moments, and then played back my recording "Jake" and also "No" could faintly be heard. I asked "Are you called Jake? Is this a trial you're in?" listening back "Jake" faintly got said again, followed by "Sailor" and "Ale".

I said on camera "I seem to have made contact with Jake, he mentions sailor and ale. I speculate this Jake could have been a sailor, maybe this isn't a man who was in court at all but enjoyed drinking in the pub? I'll ask him some more questions "Thank you so much for talking to me Jake, are you a sailor? What year is it?" waiting again a few moments I further heard "Sailor" and "War" on my digital recorder. "This is interesting, Jake for sure seems to be a sailor; and he mentions war, which I am thinking places him in the time period early in the last century perhaps?" I asked "Are you in the navy Jake?" I got no more EVP responses from Jake.

"I am going to sit on this chair next to the haunted one, let's see if a spirit wants to join me!" I focussed my camera closely on the chair; loudly and enthusiastically I called out "Please come and join me for a drink!" Still filming the chair, the cushion did seem to move ever so slightly. "Wow! There's a spirit sat right next to me! I feel static electricity making my hair stand up. Can you see that cushion? It's pressed down slightly and I caught this all on camera for you!"

A loud crashing sound came from behind the bar "Argh mon dieu! Sorry for shouting, that made me jump. That was an unexplained loud noise you all heard. I'll go across the room to see what might have made it" I walked to stand behind the bar "Look there on the floor at that beer bottle; I am sure this would never have been left on the floor like that. That bottle must have made the noise when it fell or maybe got pushed onto the floor. This is a haunted room, I can say this for sure now!"

"Argh mon dieu! Sorry again for shouting. Someone just touched my right arm! Robyn says this is happening to her customers all the time"

All these incidents occurred during the course of the hour and a half that I spent in lockdown in The Buccaneer Suite, nothing of any further significance happened after this Finishing with a piece to camera I called this investigation off "We have heard from Jake the sailor; seen for ourselves the haunted chair getting sat in; that beer bottle being thrown on the floor and I got touched on my right arm. Although nothing manifested from when this room was used as a court, I feel history all around me. Next I move on to the main bar area for my final lockdown here at Jim's Bar".

## THE MAIN BAR

I took some time out in Robyn's fragrant office to collect all my thoughts together and prepare myself for how I was going to proceed with what I knew would be my final investigation at Jim's. I wanted to get some real answers for Robyn, my viewers and also myself!

I eventually got started on this final investigation after ten o'clock. I'd never taken this approach before. I figured it would take as long as it took.

Apart from my fixed camera sat on the bar, I took no equipment with me, only my protective silver amulet and years of development as a psychic.

"I am back in the main bar area at Jim's Bar. Please never do anything as crazy as I am about to, unless you too have the same years of experience as me" I explained further "I'll be completely opening myself up to any spirit or entity in this entire building who wants to communicate with me! We know my other two investigations here left us too many questions, I next want to get us all some answers!"

I added "If I sense anything, I'll say it all out loud for you as it psychically comes to me, then you can get some idea of what's happening. Please understand that not everything I say will always make sense" I laughed "Probably nothing new there then!"

I stood stock still right in the middle of the customer area, my camera sat before me on the bar. Closing my eyes I put myself into the waking meditation I use when I am doing psychic work with the need to heavily protect myself from any spirits who might want to harm me. I reached out into the whole building. During the next twenty minutes, with a minute or more's gap between each of these statements, looking back later on my camera I know that I said "I am sensing multiple spirits. Don't all speak at once! Oh I see. Oh my, really? Oh this is awful. I am so sorry!" I fell silent. I opened my eyes but was clearly still in communication with an unseen spirit "I understand. Yes. I will explain. Your story will be told"

I was then back myself again "I know everything. I am going to take a short break and then I'll explain, be back with you all in a few moments!" I drank some water, and after the psychic experience to ground myself, I took on a small amount of food in the form of one of the grain and seed bars I always carry in my backpack; only then I returned to the main bar.

I placed my camera on one of the tables, sat myself down in a chair and pressed record "I know precisely what went on here one hundred and fifty years ago. This bar was used for Shanghaiing men into becoming sailors against their will. Girls were used to befriend men who came into the pub; their drinks were spiked and no longer thinking clearly they were led by this girl down into the cellars. A man waited for them in that same room I felt compelled to leave earlier. He coshed this drugged man on the head; when he woke up he was already on-board ship and usually far out at sea! The spirits I picked-up on here were all somehow connected to this practice. The evil spirit in the cellar was of the man who got paid to deliver these unwilling sailors to their new lives. This man got killed down in that room by a young man who fought back as he wasn't quite as drugged or drunk as they imagined. This young man Jake was tried in the court in this same building and he got hung for his trouble; nevertheless his actions brought an end to this pub getting used for Shanghaiing"

I added "This is an incredible story and suddenly everything makes sense. The case becomes so clear, everything relates to this practice of Shanghaiing!"

And with that I finished my filming at Jim's Bar.

## RELEASED

I texted Robyn to let her know I was all finished with my investigation at just before 11pm. While I waited for her I enjoyed some of the wine she left for me; it was excellent. Robyn arrived in half an hour; by which time admittedly half the wine was gone.

Robyn made quite the entrance as she walked into her bar, looking effortlessly sophisticated in a dazzling white mini-dress accentuating her lithe tanned body. She's already tall, now she wore high enough heels to bring her right up to my height and she'd put her long hair up in a tight high bun revealing a constellation of blue stars tattooed from behind her left ear continuing just under her hairline across to fill out the nape of her neck surrounding a small pentacle. I knew now why she gave me the knowing look when we first met and I shared my philosophy on life. Robyn's heady perfume smelled exquisite. She asked "Was your investigation fruitful?" I stood taking her in. We found ourselves looking at one another in unashamed mutual admiration for what seemed like an hour but was probably under a minute. I eventually replied "Yes Robyn, I solved all the mysteries I think" and added "But that will all have to wait until I've edited the film. I need to see if I may have captured any spirits. Robyn, I'll come back to see you next Saturday afternoon as I promised for the premier of the video before I post it up to my channel" Robyn answered "Perfect and thank you Om!"

Robyn added "Oh no Om look at the time, by now you will have missed your last train! You had better come back home with me instead to stay over for the night" I wiped all thought of taxis from my mind; well how could I possibly refuse Robyn's such kind offer?

ROBYN'S FILM PREMIER

Two days later I got busy on my laptop reviewing all of the footage from my three lockdowns at Jim's Bar. Diligently watching everything back several times to check if anything unusual got captured. During my cellar investigation in the first room I ventured into, the old cell, twice orbs of light were clearly visible moving up the wall behind me. Other than that, all the other film was exactly as I saw it with my own eyes on the day. I began the complex and enjoyable task of editing it all together to make another case video.

I continued working on the video and by the evening on Thursday it was all completed. I watched it back a few times and knew this video took what I do onto a new level. This case was complex. Working systematically and instinctively I solved it; and my client got precisely what she wanted, which was to know more about her ghosts.

The arrangement was I would visit Jim's that Saturday afternoon to show Robyn the promised premier of the video. Walking into Jim's Bar I found Robyn sat waiting for my arrival, her face lit-up when she saw me; I could get used to that. She wasn't in her pirate gear, instead blue jeans that fitted in all the right places, paired with a black t-shirt that showed enough to make you want to see more; the beautiful woman looked effortlessly sexy. Robyn got me a drink and we adjourned to her fragrant office.

I turned on my laptop and played Robyn the new video featuring her bar. She put her arm on mine and declared "This is incredible Om! I honestly cannot thank you enough. So many things that happened in Jim's make sense now. You gave me everything I asked for and then some! Where you really not tempted to exorcise that ghost in the cellar?" I smiled "No Robyn, I made you a promise I would leave them all be; as long as I don't need to ever go back down there into that cellar all is good!" Robyn laughed her gentle gift from the goddess laugh; and then proved once more what I told you earlier, women are the ones who call the shots.

As I stood up to say goodbye, Robyn suggested "Om, I was just leaving for the day, would you care to come back to my place and I'll order us takeaway?" she looked me straight in the eyes and seductively added "You already know I've got the finest Bordeaux in Kent and as you are by now also aware you shall be made extremely welcome!" I answered as casually as I could "I like the way your mind works!" then I had to ask "What's that perfume you wear Robyn?" she looked a little puzzled "I never wear perfume, I use a natural odourless deodorant and then I'm good to go"

I pondered to myself that what I called 'Fragrance of Robyn' in reality must be the natural pheromones of the woman herself; I knew there and then I needed her in my life; to the woman in question I said "As they say in the movies Robyn, this could be the start of something beautiful," we both laughed…

# 2

# SUICIDE CAR PARK

"This case needs to be off the record and you cannot film"

Some of my clients like secrecy; this one took clandestine to new levels. I found myself feeling like a certain famous secret service agent when I arrived up in the North West region of England for this case; and that's as much as I can share with you about the exact location. My client this time around was a local council who definitely didn't want the news getting out that they had called on the services of a paranormal investigator, namely me. As I was to be paid for my time from out of local rate payer's public money; at the time I guessed they felt it wouldn't go down too well with these same locals to know I was in town and exactly what they were paying me for. Turned out I was right and wrong.

The email they sent said "We are aware you have previously worked for corporate clients who naturally don't wish you to make any video during the course of your investigation or indeed to divulge details of exactly what you did for them. We also fall into that category, however, in our case we are going to request an even denser veil of secrecy remains shrouded around both you and what we propose that you do for us. If you agree to these terms, we will communicate once again to inform you of your potential case"

I knew where the email originated from; they'd made no attempt to keep this secret. I admit my initial reaction was to walk far away from this one, but I didn't. What can I say; there was something about all this cloak and dagger stuff that intrigued me. I wondered how they proposed to keep secret a full-on paranormal investigation in what I could only surmise must be a public building and my involvement in the case. I get kind of noticed on the rare occasions I find myself in the throes of an investigation in full public view!

I emailed them back three days later, having taken a couple of layers of pondering through all the implications of me agreeing to their restrictive terms. It went without saying that, even if for all this secret agent stuff, if it did come out that I was in their town to conduct a paranormal investigation, some of the flack for the council's secrecy for sure would come my way. Then again I am not exactly a stranger to controversy. I agreed to their terms and waited to hear back what they had in mind; and why the need to keep everything private and only between us.

That same day I got to know what I was signing up for "We have a multi-storey car park situated above a bus station in our town. Here is a web-link to read more about it on the internet. As you will observe this once was, and occasionally still is, the favoured place for poor unhappy souls to jump off to end their lives. We want you to investigate level nine of this car park Mr Darke. There are many members of the public reporting experiencing weird things happening up there. We want you to cleanse the space for us. The need for discretion is because many relatives of the unfortunate suicides are still alive and living in the area. If it came out their local council are employing the services of basically a psychic to cleanse the place of the spirits of all their loved ones, we would be facing at the least a credibility problem and at worst become figures of hate. We don't want you to book a hotel in town in your own name; we trust in your ability to figure out how to get around this. The car park closes at 4pm on Sundays, you will have the free run of the place all evening after then. You will be given a key to afford entry to the car park whenever you are ready, which we ask you to leave in the town hall mailbox when you are through with your task"

I followed the web link to learn more about what I was taking on there. Since its construction in the late 1960's ten unfortunate souls felt the upper floor of this car park the perfect place to end their lives by jumping off. These days this would thankfully be more difficult due to the safety net topped with razor wire spanning out from the uppermost two levels; all of this didn't discourage one young woman who only five years previously somehow managed to make it past all these defences and jump to her death.

Looking at pictures of this car park I could feel the trapped souls linked to the place. I realised I'd no choice but to go there to set them free. My further contention was that once all those souls were freed, the energy of suicide would largely go with them. I hoped no further lives needed to be lost up on level nine.

I had an issue to overcome. It would be all too easy to stay out of town someplace and travel in on the Sunday evening to the car park, do my thing and then beetle-off again. Yet I knew I needed to be within the energy of the town for the entirety of my stay. Robyn came to the rescue. She took the weekend off work from Jim's Bar, and booked a hotel room for the two nights in her name. We drove on Saturday the seven hour journey from the Kent coast up to North West England together. Robyn checked in, while I waited outside in my van. After a few moments I entered the hotel, got into the lift and went up to our room. It overlooked the car park.

## THE INVESTIGATION AND ROBYN GETS HANDS-ON

This was the first time Robyn had joined me on my investigation travels. It was four months since the Jim's Bar case, after which we organically grew into being a couple. When I explained to Robyn about the clandestine nature of this case, it had been her suggestion to book our room in her name and share some of the driving with me. Frankly this was seriously impressive to me. I do obviously get that my distressed looking old VW van isn't everyone's idea of the ideal daily driver; I am not really one for cars and it serves me well enough. I respected Robyn all the more for her failure to suggest we should travel north in her modern Fiat 500. Instead she gladly took her share of time behind the wheel during our leisurely amble up the country to the town of our destination. I soon discovered that I found it deeply and profoundly erotic watching pristinely beautiful Robyn driving my old van; we didn't get too much sleep that first night after we arrived.

It was never my intention we investigate together. What I do comes from too many years to contemplate of ghostly encounters, leading on to the inevitability of becoming a full-time paranormal investigator. Robyn admittedly did co-exist with many unseen occupants at Jim's, her request to join me later that Sunday evening up on the car park shouldn't have come as too much of a surprise, yet it still kind of did.

I do get that it's horrible to make comparisons; this still didn't stop me doing precisely that in my head. Anna had worked alongside me for two years and she knew her way around paranormal nasties, and far more crucially, she understood how to protect herself. Robyn didn't have any idea on how to protect herself from paranormal nasties. My love for Robyn left me with no decision to make. I gave her a protective silver amulet identical to my own; I'd hopefully deal with anything malevolent that we might encounter as or when required…probably!

The promised key mysteriously appeared in reception at our hotel during Sunday afternoon, together with a hand- written note explaining which door it would afford us entry to. At 6pm we arrived at the external door leading to the car park stairwell. I gingerly unlocked it, half expecting an alarm to suddenly blare into existence. Silence greeted us.

We discovered the lift to be out of order or perhaps it got switched off at night? Trying to hold our breath, Robyn and I more or less sprinted our way up the stairway stinking of stale urine to reach level nine, right up there at the top of the car park. This wasn't to be my first time venturing into a deserted car park for some paranormal investigation; I can tell you that these are some seriously spooky places when everyone else has left for the day. Exiting the door we gratefully gulped in the fresh evening air…

Robyn declared herself wishing to get directly involved with the investigation and asked me what she might do. We got interrupted before I could make any suggestions "Are you two up here looking for ghosts?" this question came from the Car Park Attendant as he was walking up the ramp cars normally used "I heard they'd given my spare keys to someone and guessed what it might all be about. I stayed around watching through my CCTV to see if anyone would turn up". Having suitably scared us both out of our skins with his unexpected arrival, he now leant back against a wall to share his own personal paranormal experiences in the car park…

Offering us each a cigarette, which we declined as neither of us smoke; lighting-up himself he began by telling us his name, which it turned out was Barry. I didn't introduce us, feeling anonymity the best policy. Barry was a small skinny man dressed in a long dayglow yellow jacket; with a few days of stubble on his chin, he wore a faded baseball cap back to front on his head. He smelled strongly of cigarettes, we subtly moved to avoid being downwind of him while he smoked; we're not mad keen on the stench of cigarettes.

Barry told his story "I've worked here five years, and I can tell you I've witnessed shadow figures out of the corner of my eye or on my CCTV looking at the ninth floor more times than I've enjoyed a pint! My job means every week day at 7pm I need to walk right through the entire car park to check everything's okay, then I lock the place up for the night. I don't usually ever come up here on my own once it's gone dark. I'm only up here now it's dark because you two are here as well! Early on in this job I clearly heard the sound of sobbing right where we are stood when I did my rounds, which I'll admit scared me stiff and since then I never linger up here for too long. I feel sort of protective of my spirits, you know?"

Barry paused to light another cigarette; he continued on with his story "You know from time to time some ghost hunters or thrill seekers come into my car park and I always tell them they're trespassing and need to leave now or I'll get the police involved. I don't want them bothering the poor spirits; they had enough trouble during their life without people poking their nose in where it's not wanted now they're dead"

Robyn said "Thank you so much for sharing your brilliant stories with us Barry and even more for taking the trouble to stay behind to do this. Please do go home and get some much earned rest, we are grateful to have met you Barry as we have so much useful information from you now. Goodnight!"

I would have just thanked the man and told him we needed the place to ourselves so could he now go! I guess it must be managing her bar staff that gave Robyn people skills so superior to mine. Barry smiled at her, thanked Robyn and agreed with her that he would like to go home. He waved and shouted goodnight to us as he opened the doorway to the stairs and it closed behind him.

And so back it was to quiet once more, with just the muted sound of traffic on the road drifting up from deep down below where we stood. Looking into the distance from our high vantage point the town looked romantic at night with all the lights panning out into before us.

We kissed, after which we discussed how we were going to proceed next. I said "Robyn we need to use the digital recorder to see if we can capture some EVPs. You should be the one to try for EVPs"

With the device turned on and held out towards the void past the outer car park wall, in her aristocratic voice Robyn asked out loud "Is there anyone up here with us?" looking at me she added "Do please talk to us. We mean you no harm".

We attentively listened for anything we might have captured as we played it back. "Who are you?" could be faintly but distinctly heard spoken on the recorder. This is the point at which Robyn basically freaked out big time…

Between uncontrollable sobs Robyn told me "My first time ever using a digital recorder and I catch an EVP! You know Om I hadn't thought through all the implications of what we are doing up here in this car park, and that we would be interacting with the spirits or souls of people who were once alive!" She continued to cry. I held her until she eventually calmed down. I truly understood exactly where she was coming from. It's all too easy to excitedly go EVP chasing without giving too much thought about the source of the responses we get. I loved Robyn all the more for her human reaction to finding herself in communication with a once vital living fellow human who now existed only as an essence of the person they once were.

Robyn explained "It felt too weird listening to this poor soul who must have felt such despair he jumped straight to his death and quite likely from that exact same spot where we were stood. And yet Om, at some level deep inside while I was busily preoccupied with being girly hysterical, I already knew I needed to know more!"

I smiled at Robyn, she was a natural born paranormal investigator. We allowed ten minutes more to let her fully recover, and got back to our investigation. This time around it was me who held the recorder. I said "My name is Om Darke; my girlfriend is Robyn Humphries. We are paranormal investigators" after pausing for a few moments I asked him "Can you please tell us your name?"

We looked at one another wondering what we might have captured this time; I pressed play and "Oh" we seemed to hear at the time. Back at our hotel I would later analyse this recording on my laptop and in fact the voice appeared to be saying "Tall".

Robyn listening to it speculated "I wonder if he tried to say a name, like maybe Paul? It could be a comment on the car park building he fell to his death from or even about you Om who asked him the question, you are a tall man!"

We would continue on with trying to get more EVP's on the night but nothing else came through.

I decided the moment had arrived to do what I came there for. I announced "I am going to cleanse the space Robyn; you can help by lighting the sage we brought along with us and wafting the smoke so it fully permeates everywhere around us. I'll chant, join in with me if you feel comfortable with it once you get the idea".

Robyn firstly decided to talk out loud to this young man we had communicated with "You know you can move on from here if you want to? Look for the light, can you do that? Find the light and then move towards it, that's right isn't it, Om?" I confirmed "Yes, move towards the light, you need to leave this place now and you can be free, you deserve this!"

After this we began our cleansing ritual proper. I never share the precise nature of what I do; I even edit my videos to leave out crucial parts of the ritual to save others from trying to copy me and finding themselves confronted with rather more than they anticipated!

The whole ritual took around thirty minutes. Robyn told me the place felt so peaceful afterwards; like all the anguish had passed away leaving behind only an overwhelming sense of calm.

We left the way we came in; I locked the door and dropped the key through the town hall letterbox. Back at our hotel I asked Robyn for her impressions having experienced her first paranormal lockdown "I was never scared Om; upset for sure, but not in any way scared. I never felt closer to you than us working together on a lockdown. How was it for you having this virginal paranormal investigator alongside you?' I kissed her and truthfully answered "Magical".

# 3

# POLTERGEIST IN STORAGE

"I have no budget to pay paranormal investigators"

I don't charge for my services. I guess you're thinking the sun must have got to me as I am not making any sense. For sure I get paid when I take on a case, but I charge for my time and never for my expertise. Any psychic, who charges for their services and not their time, is either a fool or a fake in my experience.

I make more from my video channel than I charge for my time on cases. My channel pays well, allowing me to live in the good part of town, travel whenever and wherever the mood takes me, and indulge in my taste for fine food and wine.

Having my video income also allows me to use some discretion on occasion and take on a case simply because it piques my interest, complete with the knowledge my client cannot pay me this time. If the case is reasonably local to me, I'll often help people out for no fee. This possible case couldn't have been any more local!

On the outskirts of my home town Folkestone, sits the local branch of a well-known national storage company. This case all began when our local newspaper ran a two page feature on the alleged haunting in this storage facility. They interviewed the manager, who told them stories of all kinds of weird stuff happening. Footsteps heard echoing around when the place was empty, the motion sensitive lights turning on all by themselves and unexplainable loud bangs and crashes. I decided to send an email to this troubled man.

Robyn and I had been a couple for six months but we still kept our own homes; not yet taking the obvious choice of living together. It's not that we balked at the prospect of cohabiting, but at this point we still kind of lived between one another's places, going back to our own respective homes when we knew work schedules would clash or might inconvenience one another.

Robyn phoned me from Jim's "Hi Om, did you read today's newspaper by any chance?" I told her I had. "Are you going to get involved? I mean this place is practically on your own doorstep, even walking you can be there in less than twenty minutes!" she laughed at this with her soft gentle gift from the goddess laugh. I confirmed I'd just finished emailing the manager when she called me. Robyn said "I would love to come with you on this one if it happens" I thought about this for a few seconds before replying "I am going to be filming this case if it happens Robyn, I would obviously love you to be alongside me but are you sure you feel okay about appearing in the video on my channel? Millions of people will watch it" she replied "You know me better than anyone Om, at any point do I ever come across to you as the shy, retiring kind of a woman?" I laughed at this "No. No you don't Robyn!" she happily responded "Jolly good. Then it's all settled. Love you! Bye" and with that she was gone.

In my email I suggested a lockdown for two hours on the night of his choice, giving me ample time to discover and deal with whatever lurked in the building. I already kind of guessed his head office wouldn't allow him any budget for a paranormal investigation in his facility; with this in mind I made it clear I didn't intend to charge anything for my time, if he would allow permission for me to film a video during my lockdown.

His reply came the next day.

The manager asked me for a meeting, and subject to him feeling I could be trusted, he would agree to the terms of my lockdown. The hoops that I need to jump through sometimes to do a free favour never cease to astound and amuse me!

## THE APPOINTMENT

Taking a couple of hours out from work, Robyn came along with me for the meeting. Naturally she didn't bother getting changed; the woman walked alongside me into the manager's office looking like a pirate!

The manager was extremely sceptical of our credentials as paranormal investigators. A small man who looked to be around fifty years old, he had receding hair, was a little overweight, and there were half-moon glasses perched on the end of his nose; he now scrutinised us both over these glasses. Robyn showed him the sage she planned to use for smudging, to which he replied his fire alarm was connected directly to the fire station and should it be triggered they would immediately turn-up.

I quickly explained we could deal with the ghost without using sage. I gave him the website address for my video channel and suggested to him that he might like to take a gander, while we took ourselves off for an unguided tour of his facility.

Upon arrival back in his office around twenty or so minutes later his attitude had undergone a complete one hundred and eighty degree shift. He informed us that he would be delighted to agree to a paranormal lockdown for 'Mouldy and Scullery' he laughed at his own joke; we found it more challenging to share his mirth but at least we managed to smile. As we left Robyn giggled "I don't think he knew what on earth to make of us babe! I don't imagine he gets many couples visiting respectively looking like a pirate and a model for new-age fashion!" I grinned, kissed her goodbye before she got into her car and walked back to my place.

In due course on an evening the following week, Robyn and I found ourselves quite literally locked inside the massive storage facility, with no possible means of escape, together with whatever haunted the place!

I gave Robyn a camera to film this lockdown from her perspective; and took another camera for myself to film her filming the lockdown. Well at least something like that was my idea...I think!

We stayed for fifteen minutes in reception discussing how we would film the case and what Robyn's role would be. We both wanted her to be completely and directly involved in the investigation. I filmed my introduction in reception before we headed out to see what we would see.

I spoke directly into Robyn's camera "Greetings! Welcome to another paranormal case with me Om Darke. I am not alone for this lockdown; viewers allow me to introduce my fellow investigator on this case, the rather wonderful Robyn Humphries!" I panned my camera onto her and then continued "We are locked inside a mammoth storage facility located here in Folkestone, a town located on the South East coast of England. The manager of this place asked us to deal with the poltergeist type activity he's been experiencing. Shall we begin Robyn?" She looked into my camera and said "I am ready. I cannot wait to see what we encounter!"

Setting off, Robyn filmed events on her camera, my own camera for the moment was switched off; we walked along identical corridors right across the entire ground-floor and felt nothing paranormally unusual. We found the building weird enough though!

Motion sensitive lighting meant no sooner had we walked a few metres down a corridor all the lights immediately behind us went out, leaving us constantly with the irrational fear of being followed, yet we could see nothing in the impenetrable darkness from where we just walked.

I spoke into Robyn's camera "Nothing on this ground level Robyn. We are conveniently stood by this lift; we need to investigate the upper level next, where hopefully we'll find what we are looking for".

Getting into the lift and whilst obviously keen to resolve the case, we admittedly felt nervous apprehension about what we might come face to face with when the doors automatically opened! Holding hands and also holding our breath as the doors slowly slid open, we were only met with yet another long empty corridor

We exited the lift and walked along this first corridor, and this is where things began to get rather more interesting. A spirit entity of some sort definitely occupied this level of the building...

I spoke once more into Robyn's camera "I am following my psychic instinct and this storage unit we are stood in front of feels like the centre of all the activity. I sense there is something stored inside this unit that a spirit is attached to"

Robyn and I discussed the paranormal many times. She was keen to know what she needed to do if she ever found herself wishing to exorcise a ghost. At my suggestion, we turned the camera off for a few moments. I made Robyn an offer "I am happy to step back here and let you deal with this spirit Robyn, if you feel confident doing that?" Her eyes were wide open staring at me in excitement as she replied "Oh my gosh! Yes babe, I would love to!" it was decided then. I wouldn't have made this offer had I doubted her ability to do what we came there for. Robyn was ready for this.

Robyn handed me her camera, and I switched it back on. I firstly spoke into it "Robyn is about to exorcise the spirit connected to an article within the storage unit in front of us. This spirit doesn't feel evil or malevolent, more just mischievous" Robyn said "I shall meditate and chant to promptly send this unwanted spirit away from this building"

I continued filming Robyn who professionally said "I cannot make any direct contact with this spirit, which is a shame; however I shall now send it away from here!"

Robyn began chanting, I joined in after a while following her lead. We both stood there chanting and building the energy until we sensed our work there done. As always, in the video I didn't show the whole process of the exorcism.

Making our way back down to the ground level, we awaited the manager's return to release us. As we still had half an hour to wait, we filmed a conclusion to the case, taking it in turns to speak directly to the camera explaining our own perspective and feelings on the case.

A HAPPY CLIENT

Upon the manager's return Robyn detailed what we found, explained how she dealt with it and offered him the opinion we believed the issue to be cured. She asked for him to let me know by email if anything else occurred...

Two weeks later he got in touch informing me all was quiet and offering me free publicity in the local press if I wanted. I declined his offer. I may have a couple of million followers on my video channel but they don't all live in Folkestone! I didn't feel delighted at the prospect of getting recognised as 'the ghost hunter' every single time I left my house to take a walk along the seafront or do my weekly shop.

Robyn put her house up for sale and so did I.

# The Spirits at Jim's Bar

# 4

# DEPOSITED AT THE BANK

"I want you to get rid of my _____ ghosts for me!"

I looked out of the window in my den. It was a grey Sunday morning, the kind of overcast day when the weather can't decide if it's going to bless us with torrential rain or just remain drearily gloomy. An email pinged into my inbox. This turned out to be a request from a real estate broker wanting some of my particular kind of help. I never set an exact price tag for my time. He offered me £500 an hour to solve a problem he found himself faced with.

I phoned him early afternoon the same day suggesting we meet then he could tell me all about his issue and I could decide if I wanted to get involved. He was located an hour away in the town of Maidstone, situated more or less in the middle of Kent.

I called downstairs to Robyn "Babe, there's a case, have you anything pressing to do tomorrow morning?" she walked upstairs into my den and sat herself on my knee.

"Nothing that can't wait. Where are we going Om?" I played with her invitingly untied waist-length hair as I kissed her "We're off to sunny Maidstone for a meeting at half ten!" I managed to breathlessly get my reply to her question out before we were fully occupied for the remainder of that afternoon; during which Robyn didn't think once to make any comment about the exciting prospect of a visit to sunny Maidstone in the morning...

THE MEETING IN SUNNY MAIDSTONE

We set out from our new home together, situated midway between Dover and Deal in scenic St Margaret's Bay, slightly before nine on the Monday morning. We took Robyn's Fiat 500 this time; my old van doesn't enjoy torrential rain too much and we wanted to arrive in Maidstone rather than break down somewhere on the way.

"I want you to get rid of my _____ ghosts for me!" He made this demand as Robyn and I walked through the door into his office for our meeting at the agreed time, all before allowing us any opportunity to say hello or even introduce ourselves!

The guy went by the name of Lawrence Newhouse; bizarrely the man barely looked directly at Robyn at any point during our meeting. Robyn and I frequently travel;

wherever we go in the world she always kind of attracts attention; it's not like she lives for attention but she's one strikingly beautiful woman, inevitably people do tend to notice her! Lawrence seemed to prefer to pretend Robyn wasn't there.

Lawrence was a subscriber to my channel, he'd watched the film detailing our investigation in the storage facility back in Folkestone, after which he spoke to the manager we acted for; who highly recommended Robyn and me.

Robyn asked "Can tell us more about what you would like us to deal with for you please? I know you wish us to get rid of your ghosts, we shall need more details than this to effectively do as you ask"

Without looking at her, he spoke more into the room as he answered "I sell and rent out property and I've got this building on my books belonging to a banking company. It's up there on the High Street; you must have walked past it when coming here to meet me. The place has been empty for over two years. I make no commission on unsold real estate! Trouble is nobody feels comfortable in there, the energy is too weird, puts any _____ punters off wanting to buy the place!"

This stressed looking man seemed to have a perspiration issue; sweat trickled down his face and wet patches were obvious on the under arm areas and down the back of his dark shirt. He owned a large nose which kind of dominated his face framed by an untidy mop of dark curly hair which also looked damply sweaty. He spoke with a North East England Geordie accent.

Looking back on this case I sincerely wish Lawrence to have already enjoyed a nice long history of being both stressed and sweaty before he ever encountered us and not to have reacted like he did on account of Goddess Robyn sitting before him in his office making him feel so hot under the collar; although I admit it likely was.

"Are you looking at wanting us to be doing an evening or night time lockdown?" I asked, he replied "No chance of any evening lockdown mate; I don't want to be held liable for you wandering around my building in the dark! How about you meet me at the bank next Saturday morning?" Robyn responded "Yes, we understand how it is Lawrence; we shall be there for nine on Saturday morning. Allow us three hours for our investigation."

We took a look at the building in question on our way back to the car park; thankfully it had stopped raining. We didn't pick up anything especially unusual coming back; we did agree though the building would convert nicely into a fabulous looking hotel.

## GHOSTS OF THE PAST

We arrived at nine on Saturday as agreed; Lawrence stood waiting to let us in. He then proceeded to impress upon us to be careful not to hurt ourselves in his building and added that, anyway even if we did have any kind of an accident it was surely down to our own irresponsibility so don't bother trying to sue him! With that off his chest he abruptly turned, walked out of the building, and then locked the main door behind him. All without even saying goodbye!

We stood in the bank's foyer blinking at the suddenness of finding ourselves in our lockdown; we took a few moments out to become centred enough for getting underway with our ghost hunting. We opted to both carry cameras and film this time. It felt strange to have unfettered access to an entire bank, even a long disused one like this.

I recorded my usual introduction into Robyn's camera "Greetings! This is Om Darke and the rather wonderful Robyn Humphries exploring this atmospheric former bank located in the town of Maidstone here in central Kent. The real estate agent has called us in; he tells us there's this weird feeling in the building that deters any would be buyers from lingering in here for too long. We have just three hours to solve this mystery and deal with whatever it is we discover. Robyn, tell us how you feel in here? Is the energy weird to you?"

She looked into my camera "Oh my gosh! It feels jolly weird to be in a bank behind the tellers screens. It is like we are about to be reprimanded at any moment and told to leave! Regarding anything paranormal, nothing is making itself obvious to either of us so far; although I see plenty of mice are sharing the building with us!"

I addressed Robyn's camera "We are not getting psychic responses coming from downstairs in this building. I agree with you Robyn, the place certainly hits the mark in terms of being creepy though! Look at all the papers and other evidence of its former use scattered around the floors of the corridors as we walk through. It feels like there are people still working all around us, yet we are not quite able to quite see them. Do you also get the sense of this Robyn?"

She spoke into my camera "It does indeed feel like there is activity happening all around us yet we are unable to see it. This really is a most bizarre feeling!"

This was a substantial building covering three levels, having investigated every room on the ground floor we made our way up the staircase to the first floor. Slowly we walked carefully through the entire level; lastly Robyn and I ventured up to the top floor. Nothing ghostly at all was encountered, although plenty of mice kept us on our toes. Neither of us is freaked out by mice, but we didn't want to inadvertently step on one or get up too close and personal with them for the sake of anything we might catch.

Moving back down to the ground floor we found two of the cleaner looking chairs littering reception to sit down for an on-camera conversation; to repeat more or less word for word what we'd already discussed off-camera on our way back downstairs from the top floor of the building.

Robyn addressed my camera "We know of impressions being left in buildings from previous activity, like a video playing back the same scene on repeat. Stone Memory it is known as and the theory goes that the walls of a building act like the recording device. The way we both feel like the bank still functions around us, yet not quite within our sight makes me question could this be the issue here? If this is the case I don't know quite what we ought to do next…" I responded "Robyn, I believe you just solved the mystery! Do you have plenty of sage in your backpack?" Robyn nodded and smiled into my camera in the affirmative, I continued talking "Then we know exactly what we need to do next Robyn!" That in essence covered everything we talked about off-camera as we walked down the stairs making our way back to the reception area; and it genuinely was Robyn who solved the case.

We filmed ourselves practising a complete cleansing ritual throughout the entire building, which took around a full hour in total. We took it in turns filming, as I rang a temple bell behind Robyn, she went from room to room with her sage. Everything felt much more relaxed in there afterwards. The issue was cleared.

In this case we didn't deal with a direct haunting as such; rather more like the echoing shadows of the building's past occupants still going about their usual business. We acted instinctively, which achieved the desired result.

We didn't share too much with Lawrence regarding the precise details of what we deduced or even what we did to deal with it. He wasn't someone open to much conversation, when he returned at noon to set us free, Robyn simply assured him that he shouldn't have any more issues.

To her utter shock Lawrence smiled and looked Robyn straight in the eyes as he passed across one thousand five hundred pounds in cash to her. He said "Please accept this Miss Humphries. I believe this settles my account. I can sell this _____ place now, and that's worth every pound I've just given you! Thank you for your time and it was nice to meet you both" We were stunned into silence for a moment; Robyn smiled and thanked him; then we left this strange man to it.

## NEW LIFE AND NEW LIFE GOALS

A lifestyle choice we made was to eat vegan plant-based food. Neither of us feels too at home in the kitchen, we prepare most of our meals together. Robyn wanted to be my co-investigator on future cases, which I'll admit thrilled me. She is a natural on paranormal lockdowns; and also happens to look frankly amazing on-camera! We resolved to reveal nothing about our relationship in our films; we agreed the focus ought to remain solely on our cases and not our anyway indescribable love for one another. We wouldn't end up sticking to this for too long, but it seemed like a sound plan at the time.

# The Spirits at Jim's Bar

# 5

# DEMON HUNTING AFTER MIDNIGHT

"Have you heard there's a demon in the city Mr Darke?!"

Occasionally I get recognised from my video channel, I admit am not wildly excited at the prospect of this, but it happens.

Before we get properly into this case, and where exactly I got recognised, we need to deal with an elephant in the room. My former partner in both cases and life Anna; who a year and a half earlier had left Kent to go back to her home country Czechia spending some quality time with her mum.

## ANNA KOSTROVÁ RETURNS

The email pinged into my inbox one April morning. It read "Hey Darke, long time no hear or see. I've been following your videos from over here and I've observed the sizzling chemistry between you and your posh totty. Only kidding Darke; Robyn is the zpropadený hottest girl ever and with that accent to die for; although you keep it all professional in your vids, it's obvious you're both head over heels in love. Just too cute! Anyway, I'll cut to the chase. I'm coming back to Kent. Not with the intention of having anything romantic with you ever again; no offense miláček, but OMG I'm sure you have to agree with me, we were never ever meant to be any kind of a zpropadený couple!!! If Robyn is okay with this, and if you two ever find yourself in need of the services of a demonologist, I'd love to make a cameo appearance in one of your two's cases. I'll be back next month; I've rented a holiday flat in Hythe until I've found my feet. You've got my number, but I'll understand if I don't hear from you".

This was six weeks ago. I knew that by now somewhere out there Anna Kostrová was back…

I let Robyn read the email as I didn't want any secrets between us and there was every chance we might bump into Anna around Kent. She wasn't overly concerned at the news; and told me that if we ever found ourselves with a demon to deal with we should definitely contact Anna…

## AREN'T YOU?

"Aren't you Mr Om Darke?" These words were spoken by a couple of students sat at the table adjacent to mine.

Robyn had decided that learning decoupage would be a good thing. She enrolled at College in Canterbury, the reason I found myself enjoying a cup of coffee in the student café while I waited for her to finish her mid-day class. It was deserted when I arrived; the only other customers coming in after me were a young student couple, who decided that out of the entire empty canteen, the very best place to enjoy their late lunch would be at the table next to my own!

After polishing off their meals they started chatting, offering me another coffee while they bought their own and then they put our tables together to socialize.

And so it was after a while of talking, Katherine, a pretty punk girl with bright blue hair cut into a mohawk and penchant for ripped neon clothing, asked me if I was Om Darke. I confessed that I am and after this revelation our conversation went off in a completely new direction.

Katherine asked "Mr Darke, have you heard there's a demon in Canterbury? I don't automatically believe every single claim I hear of occult or paranormal activity. I wanted to know more...

I asked "Why do you think there's a demon? Have you seen it yourself?" Billy, Katherine's equally ripped neon clothed boyfriend answered this one "There's a path that's a short cut into the city from where most of us students live in two apartment blocks. This path goes through a small wood, then on past the cemetery. None of us would use this short cut once it goes dark, erm, Mr Darke! We all go the much longer way round on the pavement running alongside the road into Canterbury centre"

I queried "So this demon is where exactly, in the woods or this cemetery?" Katherine answered "We're all too scared to venture into the woods at night; I guess it's the woods then" Billy continued "Two of our friends heard growls and felt like they were being followed, when they turned around to look they saw glowing eyes in the trees behind them!"

I initially thought they were having some fun winding me up knowing who I was; yet as they talked more I began to trust this couple genuinely believed there was a demon at large. After chatting for a while, the students informed me they needed to go off to their classes, I told them "I am going to make this demon our next case and see if Robyn and I can deal with it for you. Look out for the video on my channel!" With collective smiles and thanks, off the couple went to their classes.

## A WALK IN THE SUNSHINE

Soon Robyn arrived. Over yet another coffee I told her all about the conversation and asked for her thoughts on the matter.

Robyn said "Okay, I am going to start with assuming there might not be a demon after all and let's see where we go from there! I do actually know these small woods the students told you about. As you know babe, I did my teacher-training in Canterbury, during which time I got to know the city well. Although I never walked the footpath at night, it must feel terribly creepy, especially at the point where it passes alongside the graveyard. How about this babe? Inebriated students making their way home from pubs and clubs in the early hours of the morning might imagine all sorts of weird stuff to be lurking there on the footpath. Nocturnal animals could easily make growling noises and might well sound like creepy footsteps. Maybe some local cats are also in these woods; their glowing eyes would certainly look quite demonic to our inebriated students glancing behind thinking they're being followed"

I answered "That is more or less as what I thought as well babe" I added "I think we should opt to go and walk the footpath while it's daylight, to get a feel for the place to help us in deciding if these woods and the graveyard will be requiring any further investigation".

Robyn asked "Have we got our cameras in your van?" I confirmed we did "Then let's do this properly babe and film it, working under the assumption that it shall be a case"

I did my introduction into Robyn's camera "Greetings, I am Om Darke and alongside me is the rather wonderful Robyn Humphries. For this case we're investigating in historic Canterbury exploring the footpath there behind us. Reports reached us of a demonic presence lurking here. We have no client, we're here by choice and our mission is to make this place safe for everyone to enjoy!"

Robyn held the digital recorder out in front of her, while repeatedly asking the same two questions "Does anyone wish to talk with us?" and then "Please come forward to communicate, we mean you no harm".

I carried the camera and quickly turned it on to Robyn, as unexpectedly she proclaimed "Okay, this feels too weird. Oh my gosh! There is something awful in this wood babe! I feel it watching us. Can you also feel it?" I said "Mon dieu, for sure I also feel it Robyn; especially as we walked next to the cemetery" she continued "Babe, I get the strongest feeling this thing is so evil! Never felt anything this purely evil. Oh my gosh!" I professionally added "The energy here is powerful, evident especially to Robyn, even on such a beautiful warm sunny afternoon"

Robyn stopped, as by then we were reaching the end of the footpath and arriving at a busy road. I filmed as we listened back to discover if any EVPs had been captured. "Grrrrr!" we heard distinctly twice.

We cut filming and agreed the best plan would be to head back home to freshen-up. Have an evening meal, talk through our plan of action and return to the same location after midnight.

## AND THEN THERE WERE THREE

As we were driving home it was Robyn who finally voiced the obvious question going through both of our minds "We should contact Anna Kostrová" I briefly glanced across at her "Babe, we know that Anna is far more able to deal with something like a demon than us. Am I wrong?" I smiled as I answered "You're absolutely right Robyn. My phone is here in my top pocket, take it babe and send her a text. Ask her if she's busy tonight and if she isn't, would she like to come with us to kick the ass of a demon!"

Anna arrived at our home a little after seven in the evening. Robyn answered the door after which Anna immediately enveloped her in a massive hug, in her deep accented voice she said "OMG Krásná, you're even more like a _____ Goddess seeing you for real than you look in the videos!"

Robyn told me later that day of her first impressions upon meeting Anna; she was considerably smaller than she'd expected; Anna is a petite five feet tall; Robyn took in her pale blue eyes framed by seriously heavy gothic make-up; Anna's white foundation and fire engine red lips, along with nails matching her lips; as Robyn would discover, her dramatic look barely scratches the surface of the uniqueness of Anna Kostrová!

Back to the introductions; Robyn said "Thank you Anna. Wow I can feel your energy! Oh my gosh Anna, you are exactly like an exquisitely beautiful gothic doll!" Anna laughed delightedly at this, Robyn continued "It is good to finally meet you. Om is in the shower. Would you like coffee? By the way Anna, we shall be ordering takeaway when Om soon joins us, is pizza okay for you?" Anna responded "I adore your gothic doll simile Krásná! Yes please to the coffee, I take it black and I adore all Italian food!"

I'd finished my shower, as I got dressed I unashamedly eavesdropped on their conversation. I heard Anna's footsteps stop as she was following Robyn into the kitchen "I see Darke still has his Wiccan altar, are you okay with him being into that Krásná?" In response I know Robyn must have lifted up her hair and turned around showing Anna the nape of her neck "I had this tattoo done the day I turned twenty one, this is our altar Anna" who responded "You're cooler than I thought; blessed be Krásná" Robyn responded "Blessed be Anna" Their footsteps started again; I heard Anna move out a chair to sit herself down in our kitchen. She said "You're like the dictionary definition of the complete babe; your hair is _____ gorgeous! My God you're like too _____ sexy to be for real!!! I really hope we can be friends Krásná" Robyn laughed as she handed Anna her coffee "Carry on saying things like that to me Anna and I believe we shall easily be best friends forever!" I was reassured to hear them laughing rather than screaming. Anna is such a specific person, and I hadn't known how this might all work out. I also should explain Anna uses many Czech phrases to express herself; and loves that most people can't understand. With my own sketchy knowledge of the language I knew Anna called Robyn beautiful and was literally using this as her own name for Robyn with Krásná. I'll leave you to work out for yourself what her other phrases mean.

I walked downstairs and made my entrance. Anna hadn't changed significantly. I observed that her once brutally short blonde bob now sat not too far above her shoulders, her eyes had their slightly mad look to them and she hadn't lost her taste for tightly figure-hugging little black dresses leaving nothing whatsoever to the imagination.

## The Spirits at Jim's Bar

Anna said "Hiya Darke, good to see you. No need to look so trepidatious miláček, I promise that I'm not going to pounce on you. Anyway I fancy too sexy to be real Krásná here way more than I ever fancied you!" she laughed at her own joke. Robyn looked at me wondering if Anna was being serious, I honestly hadn't got a clue. Politely I asked her "How's your mum?" Anna replied "She's the same as ever Darke. Just like me still mad, bad and dangerous to know! She's dating this biker and got herself a Harley" I laughed "Yep, no change there!"

Anna said "Are you Libran Krásná?" Robyn answered in the affirmative. She then quite openly asked "How old are you?" Robyn replied "I turn thirty in October" Anna added "And Darke is Aquarius and thirty two; you two truly are made for each other" she said "I'm Scorpio; in eighteen months I'm hitting forty but I'll worry about that when it happens; I usually scare the living daylights out of most potential suitors!" She laughed at this. We didn't know quite how to respond and so we both ended up smiling at her. She grinned back at us her slightly mad blue eyes glinting in the artificial light through the blackness of all the make-up surrounding them.

Later that evening, after enjoying our pizzas, we brought Anna up to speed on the earlier events in Canterbury. We related my conversation with the students, and showed her the raw unedited footage of our earlier walk-through of the site. On a case Anna is still mad as a box of frogs, but she does know exactly what she's doing. I would trust her with my life, and you know maybe I even did more than once during our lockdowns back in the day. Her comments after watching through all our footage were "OMG! That's one serious demon you've found me! I'm going to zpropadený enjoy this one. I'll fully brief you both on what I plan to do and on your roles; we'll rehearse until we get it word and action perfect, okay? Hey Krásná, shall we go up to bed and relax together for a while until our lockdown?"

I said "Understood Anna, we'll follow your lead. And behave yourself!" Anna pouted "I apologise Robyn, you know I'm only teasing, right?" Robyn smiled at Anna who added "After all it's not like I'm some bi chick into zpropadený sexy babes like you; well you know perhaps I might just occasionally make an exception, but strictly only on days ending with the word day!" we all laughed. Anna hadn't changed one bit.

A moment later Anna unexpectedly began to cry, which certainly shocked the both of us. Robyn held her and asked "What is it Anna? Do you want talk about it?" She replied "I lost my dad when I was only five years old Robyn. I know he's looking out for me. I feel this so strongly Robyn! I live recklessly because I know no harm can possibly come to me. My dad makes sure of it!" I said "I feel this to be true Anna, I know he is with you always" she replied "I miss him Darke" I answered "I know Anna, I know".

Anna laughed, the moment now passed "What must I zpropadený look like? I'm off to your bathroom straight away to clean up my face and immediately re-do my eyes; this might take some time!"

We talked. We planned. We prepared.

Night-time paranormal investigations are not something I ever specifically set out to get involved with; if there's some spirit to be found at a location it doesn't generally bother waiting around until the sun sets to get on with its business of haunting. Spirits are often reported witnessed at night as our senses are more naturally alert then; and so what might very well have been happening anyway in broad daylight, we suddenly become far more aware of once the sun has set.

## MEETING THE DEMON AT 3AM

We arrived back at the footpath in Canterbury a little after 2am…

We each carried a protective amulet. I designed these years ago and got a silversmith to make them. As several dozen got made, Anna was able to once more have her own. We were armed with compact powerful LED torches, Anna had the digital recorder; Robyn and I each carried a video camera, set on night vision.

There were two reasons for our night time paranormal investigation.

One, there were less likely to be too many people around, meaning we would all be free to deal with the demonic creature without much chance of any interruptions.

Secondly, all the reported cases of demonly encounters had occurred late at night or early in the morning!

I half whispered my case introduction to our lockdown into Robyn's camera "Greetings from me Om Darke, back at the footpath in Canterbury we visited earlier during daylight, it is now 2am. With me as usual is the rather wonderful Robyn Humphries; and we have a surprise special guest for this case. Anna Kostrová is back! Former resident demonologist Anna has returned to the fold for this case to lend her expertise in dealing with this entity. Welcome back Anna, what are we aiming to achieve tonight?" Speaking into my camera Anna said "Guys, this is going to get extreme! We're prepared and ready to take on this demon. We all agree this case isn't closed until Canterbury is free of this entity!"

We took a moment to prepare ourselves before heading down the footpath. Holding hands we stood in a circle, and called upon our guardian goddess to protect us against anyone or anything that meant us harm. Anna was already long familiar with this protection ritual, and although she knew her dad would protect her, she did tell us she for sure felt safer after the formality of our ritual.

Anna led the way, I walked alongside panning across to her with my camera, Robyn shadowing closely behind us filming from her perspective. Robyn told me later at that moment, before anything happened, how she thought to herself how quiet and peaceful the woods seemed; she wouldn't have to wait too long for that to all change. We observed the woods were utterly pitch dark, we literally couldn't see our own hand in front of our faces. We all agreed before setting off into the woods we didn't really want to use our torches other than to illuminate anything unusual we saw to debunk it or if not debunking, then obviously investigate further. We found we constantly needed to keep on briefly illuminating our way with the torches, otherwise we would never be able even see our fellow investigators never mind about navigating our way between all the trees without walking straight into them!

Anna continued leading the way, suddenly she stopped dead, putting one finger to her lips and with her other hand another finger pointing at her ear, signifying we needed to listen. We could all clearly hear the sound of branches getting pushed through by someone or something. With our torches switched off, we peered into the darkness trying to get some sense of the direction the noises originated from. Which appeared to be from somewhere over to our right; as one all three of us pivoted to look in that direction.

We clearly saw glowing red eyes looking straight at us from a distance of around twenty metres! We certainly all knew what the risks were when simultaneously all three of us set off walking directly towards the red eyes; which faded as we neared the point where they had been.

Anna confirmed, as if this needed any confirming, what we just witnessed was definitely the demonic entity! Anna whispered into Robyn's camera "I really hope your camera picked that up Robyn; we all clearly saw eyes through the trees, they were red and glowed! As we arrived at the spot the eyes were gone; at least we know for sure the demon is at large here. We need to carefully plan our next move"

By torchlight we gingerly made our way through the trees and back onto the main footpath. Robyn spoke quietly into my camera "We need to find this anomaly, this creature. You all witnessed it ran away from us scared! It must have some den close by and next we shall find this den. Anna and Om let us hunt down this demon and finally deal with it!" Robyn told me after the case she said these words of bravado for the benefit of our audience, but in reality felt fearful at the prospect of actually doing for real what she had just suggested; this would be Robyn's first encounter with a demon; it never gets old believe me!

The woods were eerily silent now, not even the sounds of nocturnal wildlife could be heard. We continued slowly walking. Were we scared? Oh heck yes and quite a lot; well maybe not Anna, she seemed to be enjoying herself; but Robyn and I were scared for sure, yet we both knew that we needed to do this otherwise we might as well stop right then identifying as paranormal investigators.

The graveyard always stood out as our destination that night. By and by it appeared there on our left hand side. Anna whispered into my camera "The malevolent psychic energy emanating from out of this cemetery is palpable to all of us" she further whispered "We know we need to go in there; we are ready aren't we Robyn and Darke?" We both agreed we were. I then spoke to Robyn's camera "This demon will be fully aware why we're here and it's going to be distinctly displeased with us. Without any doubt at all, this thing will attack us!" adding "We're protected, and we need to remember this at all times. We cannot allow fear to take us over; it will feed off any fears leaving us incredibly vulnerable"

Anna whispered into my camera "Are you both ready? Okay, we'll take a few moments to compose ourselves. Robyn, I promise to keep on holding onto your hand whatever is happening. Right beautiful people, let's do this!"

We walked confidently to the entrance of the graveyard; pushed open the gate, which appropriately squeaked right on cue like some horror movie cliché; but this wasn't a fictional movie, this was our all too real investigation and we knew things were about to get a whole lot more serious and equally that there was no going back. We were now committed.

## THE DEMON

"Growl!" We all heard the unmistakable call of the demon. "Growl! Growl!!!" I do get what we did next would quite likely seem crazy to most people. We changed direction heading slowly and deliberately straight towards where we sensed the growls emanated from. The hunter had become our prey!

Our world suddenly turned a whole lot bleaker as it attacked. And it threw everything it could at us. Trying to bring all our fears to the surface; as it simultaneously attempted to physically attack us. Our heavy protection kept us safe. Of the three of us, only Anna could literally see this demon; stood there about three metres away apparently astride a grave.

Speaking into Robyn's camera Anna quickly said "Around two metres tall, more or less humanoid in shape, horns on its head, red glowing eyes, the creature is practically a shadow figure; in this pitch blackness I find myself unable to penetrate through all that darkness enough to be really be able to see any defined features or if it wears clothes".

It continued to attack us full on. Gale force wind nearly pushed us off our feet; all we could see around us was this cloying darkness. The demon continually growled in its annoyance. Robyn and I couldn't actually see the creature but we were for sure in no doubt of its presence!

Robyn said quietly into her own camera "Every fear I ever have ever known, every of my self-doubts, every decision I ever regretted comes back to haunt me in a massive wave of negative emotion. I struggle rather a lot with this!" As promised, Anna reassuringly kept on holding tightly onto Robyn's hand, which gave her strength. Robyn added into her own camera "I know because of Anna I am safely protected from whatever the demon can throw at me!"

As the cacophony of noise began to reach a crescendo "We zpropadený need to do this right now people!" Anna yelled.

We commenced chanting together in Latin as Anna had us rehearse until word perfect before setting out that night. We each threw a handful of the powdered selenite Anna prepared straight at this anomaly. We moved forward holding hands and began to shout out the magical words together; as one voice we called upon all four natural elements one by one to banish this demon back to where it came from. Through the power of each element and finally by the power of our Guardian Goddess we all ordered the demon gone…now!

The case was over, off went our cameras. I said I would later explain in voice-over for our viewers what happened in the finale of us banishing the demon and how it felt when it suddenly went. We group hugged in relief…as all fell silent.

SILENCE

After a few moments the silence was broken by the sound of dozens of bats suddenly swooping and flying all around us. We heard owls hooting in the woods adjacent to where we stood. Somewhere in the near distance a dog barked.

Feeling drained, we sat down on a bench in the graveyard to recover some of our energy before returning home. The now clear night allowed us to make out details on some of the graves around us. We heard the sound of footsteps; looking out towards the path we saw an elderly gentleman gently strolling past taking his little dog for a nocturnal walk. Neither of them noticed us.

Glancing at her phone, Robyn announced it to be shortly after 3am; how appropriate 'The Witching Hour'. Anna still held onto Robyn's hand; she turned towards her and holding her head with her other hand she passionately kissed Robyn full on the lips for well over a minute; after which she let her hand go. Robyn looked bemused more than anything; but said nothing. We left to head back to Folkestone.

DEBRIEFING

We all spent most of the following morning resting to recover. Anna slept over in one of our guest bedrooms rather than travelling back to her own place. She was the first of us up, and made Robyn and me coffee. Sitting on the edge of our bed she shared with us her feelings about events the night before "The connection and chemistry between you is right off the scale, you only need to look at each other to know exactly what the other one is thinking. I mean zpropadený wow! I know this may be my only cameo alongside you but I totally loved it! No offence to you Darke, but Krásná brings something magical to the table. This was way better and more enjoyable than any of our old cases Darke!" She concluded "Krásná, I was full of adrenalin please forgive me girl; looking at you as we sat on that bench I got overwhelmed with the desire to _____ kiss you properly at least once; if this is any consolation to you Krásná you are the _____ sexiest hottest girl I ever kissed in my life!"

Robyn smiled "I understand Anna, I honestly really do. I was also full of adrenalin; believe me there are far worse experiences than getting kissed by you! Thank you for so determinedly holding onto my hand Anna, this was my first time facing a demon and you helped me more than you will ever know; if the price for you helping me was kissing with you in a graveyard I think I got a good deal!" we all laughed and Anna looked relieved. Robyn added "Anna, I would adore to work with you on another case, you're hilarious to hang out with; and it turns out you are my absolute favourite beautiful gothic doll!" Anna laughed and said "That is such a relief to me, thank you! I honestly thought you would both _____ hate me" You might be wondering what I made of 'the kiss'. I saw it in context as meaning nothing, and only the result of left-over adrenalin from the case, there really was nothing to forgive Anna for.

I also smiled at her "Don't be so sure this is your last cameo Anna; we both enjoyed working with you and adored the different dynamic you brought to the team. I know you need to fit things in around your new life in Kent, but, should you be available for any other demonic cases we would love to have you once again alongside us Anna!"

Anna turned her slightly mad gaze full upon us "Ano prosím! In other words; yes please!" she added "Take it from me you need to get married. Don't zpropadený question me why, but you must get married! You'll know why after".

## THE POSSESSED BOOK

We bought an early hardback copy of the classic Zolar's Encyclopaedia and Dictionary of Dreams in a second hand bookstore on Monday next. This book would definitely be one to make it into our rapidly expanding library.

That is when things started getting rather weird in our home. We loved our home precisely because there wasn't anything even slightly ghostly, paranormal or unusual with the energy; we needed a place like this as a home base, it felt wonderful to relax in the chilled energy after a busy day. Robyn still owned her pub but left the day to day running to her manager and only went in three days a week just to keep an eye on things, now sans any pirate gear; okay admittedly she did still don it occasionally but only in the privacy of our own home…

We found suddenly a maelstrom of awful energy made us both feel like we were in the eye of a storm. We couldn't sleep properly and frankly couldn't wait to get out of the door to someplace else every morning.

After a whole long week of feeling uncomfortable in our own home, over lunch in our favourite vegan café in Deal, we finally shared a conversation about this.

Through tears Robyn said "Babe, I think we are going to need to be moving home soon". I responded "How can this place have once felt so amazing and now feel like we live in some portal to hell?"

Having thought for a few moments I added "Look Robyn, something must have changed in there in this last week! What is different?" We sat there in silence thinking back over what we'd done and if anything different could be causing us to feel so uncomfortable.

"Mon dieu it's got to be down to that book!" this was me. "What book?" came back Robyn" I explained "That dream book Robyn! It's the only thing that's different since last week; it must be that!"

We sprinted the two miles back home. Quickly finding the book we hadn't even opened yet to look at, Robyn grabbed it to run flat-out from our home. She threw it straight into the nearest public litter bin. Returning after only a few moments to find me stood in the middle of our living room with my eyes closed. "Well?" Robyn asked "Yep, it was the book babe" as I flopped myself down on our sofa. We once more felt at peace in our home.

## WANTING TO SEE MORE OF ANNA

I edited together all the various pieces of our filming from Canterbury; which ended up being one impactful video, in fact likely the most impactful so far posted to my channel.

Comments ranged from amazement about what we did on the night; questions asking for more details from Anna wanting to know what exactly seeing a demon feels like; but most enthusiastic of all were the hundreds of posts in praise of Anna being a part of the case, and asking if she was now back as permanently part of the team.

Over the course of the week from posting DEMON HUNTING AFTER MIDNIGHT, my channel acquired nearly a million more new subscribers.

The videos were generating serious income. If anyone else appears in any one of my lockdown videos I ensure that the revenue from it is equally shared between us. Anna had enough income from those two years spent alongside me to pay the rent for her flat and live quite comfortably. Robyn and I bought our home not too far from mortgage-free; on account of obviously selling our own two homes, but also with revenue from my channel.

## THE NEXT CHAPTER

An American paranormal magazine vlog, based on the same video hosting site where we post our vids, got in touch with me wanting to interview us after this case.

Recognising that this would expose us to a whole new audience, and never having been interviewed about our cases before, once I was happy with the deal on offer, I said yes.

They wanted Anna to also be a part of the interview, which would for sure be interesting for their viewers!

In the following chapter, THIS TIME IT'S PERSONAL is the complete and entire transcript of this interview.

ns at Jim's Bar

# 6

# THIS TIME IT'S PERSONAL

Matt - Hi I'm Matt Iommi for Ghostly Goings-On Magazine; I'm delighted to be talking today with three cutting-edge guys of the paranormal world Om Darke, Robyn Humphries and Anna Kostrová. This team make ground-breaking films featuring their own paranormal lockdowns!

All of us at once - Hi Matt!

Matt – Mr Darke, Anna and Robyn good to talk with you. Let's start with your name Mr Darke; where did that come from?

Me – It genuinely is my name Matt! I get it might sound like I made it up. My dad is from Folkestone on the Kent coast here in England; Darke is a local surname going all the way back to 1066 and the Norman Conquests.

Matt - Wow! That's too cool; I guess you couldn't have a better surname as a paranormal investigator, huh?

We all laugh.

Matt – You got any siblings Mr Darke, and if so, are they also involved in the paranormal?

Me – I have one brother; twelve years younger than me. Zen lives with our parents and he's at University. He's studying to be a civil engineer.

Matt - Anna you re-joined the team recently, how long had you already known the other two guys?

Anna – I met Darke around four years ago and we did some stuff making lockdown vids for a while. Robyn I met the first time on the DEMON HUNTING AFTER MIDNIGHT case.

Matt – And you're an expert on demons Anna, how did that happen?

Anna – I've experienced so many weird things in my life; demonology became my special area of interest way before I made any videos. They called me in for this case they were working on because they knew dealing with a demon would be central to resolving it. You don't go to college to study demonology Matt, it comes from life experiences!

Matt – Robyn; you and Anna are the two girls in the team, how does that work in terms of the dynamic between the two of you? Is there ever any rivalry?

Robyn - Anna and I work in different ways and that works in the interests of the case. Anna brings her own dynamic to the team and she is utterly hilarious to work alongside! I totally adore Anna; she is like my petite big sister, she looks out for me.

Anna –I have so much respect for Robyn, and it's never about competing, we complement one another. During this case Robyn and I were constantly looking for new ways we could combine our gifts to work together. Robyn has this sprinkling of fairy dust that makes her magical to be around. She is the classic psychic; whereas I'm more attuned to the dark side!

We all laugh.

Matt – Our viewers can all see you're one good looking dude Mr Darke, and there alongside you are these two freakin' red hot girls! Anna, do you think that you girls and your sizzling looks have helped you gather so many followers?

Anna – That is so not a cool question Matt! I hope you're playing devil's advocate and not quite serious; only out of politeness I'll answer this. I know all our amazing followers and subscribers are there because they're into our cases. I mean we're not in some pop band needing to look 'hot' to sell records; we're three serious paranormal investigators Matt.

Robyn – What a question Matt! It makes our followers seem rather shallow. There are thousands of channels chock-full of 'freakin' hot' and 'sizzling' girls; anyone who is into that can tune into. We make paranormal lockdown films.

Me – Anna and Robyn are not girls, they're women; and you know Matt they just proved that to you when they offered you dignified responses to what was frankly a silly question!

Matt – Guys I hear what you're saying and yeah you got me! Kudos and respect to you Anna and Robyn for answering my dumb ass question. I love the way you all support one another, so freakin' cool!

Matt – Mr Darke, your cases are all based in England. Have you ever worked in another country or would you consider this?

Me – We are open to the idea, yes for sure. Get in touch to make us interesting offers viewers, and we'll consider them!

Anna and Robyn nodded and smiled in agreement with me.

Matt – So what next for you or can't you talk about your upcoming cases?

Robyn – Not everything we do gets filmed. There are some sensitive situations or clients who prefer us not to make any video. We have some cases coming up Matt. Do keep on watching our channel for the latest ones!

Matt – I have one final question which I always ask my guests; I would like each of you to answer me in turn if you could? Where do you see yourself in ten years' time? Anna first off.

Anna – As honestly as I can answer, I don't know Matt. I live in the moment.

Matt – Robyn.

Robyn – I am sure that what are doing now shall remain an important part of our lives, in what exact form and how this literally manifests, who can say?

Matt – Mr Darke.

Me – I think we'll do many new things in the next ten years Matt. There will always be the paranormal and there will always be new locations to investigate. Watch this space as they say!

Matt – Thank you once again to all of you for being my guests today! Next I get up close and personal with the team, as I go solo with firstly Mr Darke and then each of these two gorgeous girls; apologies, I mean these two gorgeous women! As we talk about life, love and the paranormal; keep on watching folks, you're not gonna want to miss this!

Anna – Thanks Matt, on behalf of all of us, it's been fun!


INTERVIEW WITH OM DARKE

Matt - Hi I'm Matt Iommi for Ghostly Goings-On Magazine; it's my pleasure to be talking today with Mr Om Darke. He makes up one third of a paranormal investigation team making ground-breaking films featuring their lockdowns.

Me – I am happy to be talking with you Matt.

Matt – Great to be talking with you Mr Darke. Ghostly Goings-On Magazine subscribers came up with a set of questions they'd like each member of the team to answer, I'm gonna be asking all of you three exactly the same questions. You ready Sir?

Me – Go for it Matt!

Matt – Mr Darke, when did you first become interested in the paranormal?

Me – From as early as I can remember. I spent the first half of my childhood growing up in the remote French countryside. My father inspired my interest in all things spooky Matt. He was a paranormal investigator back in France, I would follow all his cases, he told me that one day I would do more than he ever did. I guess he was right.

Matt – That's cool your dad inspiring and encouraging you. Okay, next question, which I think has a fairly obvious answer after what you just told me. Where are you from Mr Darke?

Me – I was born in the Normandy region of France. I visit regularly, most of my extended family live there. The later part of my childhood I spent in Kent, which is where I lost any trace of a French accent.

Matt – Looking back on your early cases, is there anything you would change if you could, like maybe in terms of what you did or how you dealt with a case?

Me – Not really. Life is about learning.

Matt – Mr Darke what's the most scared you've ever been during a lockdown?

Me – To be honest Matt I am never so scared I can't be doing what I came to the location for. This case last year I investigated with Robyn, POLTERGEIST IN STORAGE was scary enough. The lights kept on going off while we were walking round and this creeped us out quite a bit.

Matt – I watched that video Sir and you're one cool dude under pressure, I had no idea you were getting freaked out in there man! Next question Mr Darke. Do you have a girl or boyfriend and if you do, what do they think of what you do for a living?

Me – Robyn Humphries is my life partner! We met when I investigated her bar and we majorly fell for one another; we've been a couple ever since. It's challenging to convey in words Matt how much I love that incredible woman mind, body and soul!

Matt – Wow man that's way too cool! Robyn looks like a freakin' Greek Goddess man and talks exactly like your Brit actress Emma Thompson. You're one freakin' lucky guy dude! Next question. Do you ever get recognised in the street?

Me – It happens. We never film our cases for the fame, we know viewers enjoy watching them and we enjoy making them. I do get that if people recognise me they're usually going to want to ask some questions. I give them whatever time I can spare.

Matt – Is there any one location on your wish list for going on a lockdown?

Me – The Empire State Building!

Matt – Are there any other paranormal teams you would like to work with?

Me – Not really Matt. I love Robyn; and after all Anna is rather unique!

Matt – Would you ever go solo into a haunted house?

Me – I still do solo lockdowns occasionally. Yes.

Matt – What do you like to do when away from the paranormal?

Me – I meditate. Robyn and I are Pagan and Wiccan. I adore spending as much time as possible with Robyn, we travel a lot visiting art galleries pretty much around the world; oh and I am also a fourth dan black-belt in Taekwondo.

Matt – Wow! Really? I'll make sure I don't annoy you Sir! If you weren't a paranormal investigator what would you be doing?

Me – Oh that's an interesting question! I never gave that one much thought. What would I be doing? Let me give you a considered answer rather than a sound-bite Matt. I believe I would be teaching meditation or Taekwondo.

Matt – I'm through with the questions Mr Darke. Thank you for being so open with me.

Me – I want to ask you a question Matt. How did you get into doing this job?

Matt – I worked on student radio, when I left Uni I got a job as junior reporter on a small cable news channel and then I got offered this job. It's cool getting to meet and talk with so many interesting people like you; and from all around the world.

Me – Okay, thank you again for having us Matt.

Matt – You've all been magical, thanks Mr Darke and you need to all come back on here sometime! I'll talk with you later about it.

## INTERVIEW WITH ROBYN HUMPHRIES

Matt - Hi I'm Matt Iommi for Ghostly Goings-On Magazine; it's my pleasure to be talking today with Robyn Humphries. She makes up one third of a paranormal investigation team making ground-breaking films featuring their lockdowns.

Robyn – Hello Matt.

Matt – Good to talk with you Robyn. Ghostly Goings-On Magazine subscribers came up with a set of questions they'd like to hear each member of the team answer, I'm gonna be asking you three exactly the same questions. You ready Robyn?

Robyn – As I'll ever be!

Matt – Robyn, when did you first become interested in the paranormal?

Robyn – I own a seriously haunted bar. It is rather difficult to ignore the paranormal when it is such a part of one's everyday work environment. I used to be in there full-time, however since paranormal investigations became a part of my life, I now leave the day to day running to my manager.

Matt – You look like this freakin' goddess and you own an English pub?! Wow! Your accent really is something else Robyn, I could sit listening to you talking all day! You do know you sound exactly like Emma Thompson, right?

Robyn – Thank you Matt. That has been suggested to me more than once. Personally I cannot hear it.

Note: Robyn sounded precisely like Emma Thompson as she denied sounding like Emma Thompson!

Matt – Okay Robyn, next question. Where are you from?

Robyn – Kent in England.

Matt - Looking back on your early cases, is there anything you'd change if you could, like maybe in terms of what you did or how you dealt with a case?

Robyn – I don't think I would Matt. After all, life is all about learning.

Matt – Wow Robyn! That's more or less word for word what Om Darke said when he answered that question! What's the most scared you've ever been during a lockdown?

Robyn – Investigating the demon in our latest case! This did scare me considerably. Anna looked after me on the night; she had my back and helped me to get through it.

Matt – Next question. Do you have a boy or girlfriend and if you do, what do they think of what you do for a living?

Robyn – Yes Matt, I am in a relationship with Om Darke. One's life-partner must accept us for exactly who we are. I have Om who loves me unconditionally for who I am; and of course I feel precisely the same way about him. It is challenging to convey in words our relationship; I love that man mind, body and soul.

Matt – He's a fortunate guy Robyn! You're one freakin' beautiful woman; I really mean it babe, you're so freakin' gorgeous! Om Darke said almost just the same when he described how he feels about you? Next question; do you ever get recognised in the street?

Robyn – Matt, a woman is not some prize to be gained and then the man is to be congratulated upon claiming her as his own. Our love transcends anything like the considerable physical attraction we each possess for one another or enjoying spending every possible moment in another's company like we do, we are soulmates and feel blessed to love one another! To finally answer your question Matt; I never get recognised that I am aware of. Om does, but not me yet. I am grateful we have millions of subscribers, but that's from all around the world, not in the area where we live!

Matt – Is there any one location on your wish list for going on a lockdown?

Robyn – The Empire State Building would be cool!

Matt – Are there any other paranormal teams you would like to work with?

Robyn – No.

Matt – Would you ever go solo into a haunted house?

Robyn – Why would I want to do that? I get involved in cases if we are invited and then only alongside Om; or as on our last case, with Anna as well.

Matt – What do you like to do when away from the paranormal?

Robyn – I am fortunate to live by the coast in Kent, I love walking on wild days watching the waves crash in on the beach. I am a long time meditator and into yoga Matt; no pun intended! Om and I are Pagan and Wiccan. We enjoy travelling to numbers of locations around the world visiting art galleries.

Matt – If you weren't a paranormal investigator what would you be doing? I guess running your pub, yeah?

Robyn – More than likely; although teaching Art in High School piqued my interest and I got my teaching degrees. I did teach for a few years, until Jim's Bar came into my life.

Matt – I'm through with the questions Robyn. Thank you for being so open with me and our viewers.

Robyn – It has been quite my pleasure Matt.


INTERVIEW WITH ANNA KOSTROVÁ

Matt - Hi I'm Matt Iommi for Ghostly Goings-On Magazine; it's my pleasure to be talking today with Anna Kostrová. She makes up one third of a paranormal investigation team making ground-breaking films featuring their lockdowns.

Anna – Good morning, afternoon or evening depending on when you're watching. Hi to you Matt!

Matt – Good to talk with you to Anna. Ghostly Goings-On Magazine subscribers came up with a set of questions they'd like to hear each member of the team answer, I'm gonna be asking you all exactly the same questions. You ready Anna?

Anna – I'm always ready miláček!

Matt – I bet you are! Anna when did you first become interested in the paranormal?

Anna – This goes back to my home country when I was only small and I became firstly aware of weird energies in older buildings; I became fascinated to know all about demons. As a psychic I'm well attuned to sense negative spirits.

Matt – That's kind of darkly erotic Anna, but here at GGOM we love darkly erotic! Next question. Where are you from?

Anna – I was born in Prague. I moved to London aged eight. I always identify firstly as a Czech woman but I adore England, it's a cool place to live. I'm now based in Kent.

Matt – Your accent is freakin' sexy! This next question is I'm not too sure is relevant to you Anna, you only recently re-joined the team after quite the time out; I'll ask you anyway and answer if you like. Looking back on your early cases, is there anything you would change if you could, like maybe in terms of what you did or how you dealt with a case?

Anna – On our latest case I wish I'd worn flats instead of heels. I'm like some kid stood next to Darke and Robyn, they're zpropadený giants compared to me! I decided to try and look more proportional to them and heels were a zpropadený stupid decision for exploring in a wood at night. My bad!

Matt – Okay Anna, I'll take on board this advice if I ever go hunting for a demon in some woods at night!

They both laugh.

Matt - What's the most scared you've ever been during a lockdown?

Anna – I love kicking the ass of zpropadený demons! I don't scare easily miláček!

Matt – Do you have a boy or girlfriend and if you do what do they think of what you do for a living?

Anna – I'm not in any relationship right now.

Matt – No way! Really?! That's freakin' insane man!

Matt seems transfixed by staring at Anna on his webcam.

Matt - Sorry folks got a bit distracted there for a moment. Do you ever get recognised in the street?

Anna – I'm not like Katy Perry; I'm just this zpropadený demon hunting chick appearing in paranormal videos. I don't get recognised in the street.

Matt – I love a hot sexy woman in glasses! Is there any one location on your wish list for going on a lockdown?

Anna – They're not here on my face for fashion Matt, they help me to see! On paranormal investigations and actually most of rest of time I wear contacts. Today I felt like looking intellectual; and apparently I still don't!

The both laugh.

Anna – Stonehenge.

Matt – Are there any other paranormal teams you would like to work with?

Anna – No. I love Robyn and Darke like family.

Matt – Would you ever go solo into a haunted house?

Anna - I went off into many haunted locations solo before I hooked up with Darke strictly professionally to make some lockdown videos the first time around; now I would take my 'family' along with me!

Matt – What do you like to do when away from the paranormal?

Anna – I windsurf. You know Matt; there are naturist beaches in Kent where I don't need to even bother with any _____ bikini? I adore the feeling of the air, sun and sea on my naked body. I zpropadený live for that!

Note: Anna made this 'fact' up on the spot. She loves doing that kind of thing, it amuses her. Matt's mouth falls open at this completely untrue revelation; I guess he was visioning Anna on her naturist beach in his mind; he is temporarily lost for words. Eventually…

Matt – You heard of Goldie Horn? You've got that kooky sexy thing going on she had back in the day; but you're way freakin' hotter than her!

Anna – For sure I know who Goldie Horn is and I'll take that one; thanks miláček! How about we get back to the official questions Matt?

Matt – Sorry Anna. My final question is this, if you weren't a paranormal investigator what would you be doing?

Anna – Fashion designer, if I could be bothered with going back and finishing Uni. I do make a lot of my own clothes.

Matt – I'm through with the questions Anna. Thank you for being so open with me.

Anna – That was interesting on so many levels! Nice talking with you Matt, bye everyone!

AFTERNOTE

As promised, the editors promptly emailed me our copy the video of this interview for our channel and for some reason I didn't get around to posting it for well over a year. Okay, I confess that I am not being totally honest with you here. It was all because of Anna! The interview left viewers with the impression Anna is a regular part of the team. I didn't want our followers wondering where Anna is; and questioning us about her absence every single time Robyn and I made a new case video.

I finally posted it a few weeks before we headed up to an adventure in Scotland, but that's all for much later. Before then, next it's time for you to meet my twin...

# The Spirits at Jim's Bar

# 7

# THE HAUNTED APARTMENT

All of my cousins are French!

I sense what you're thinking; no I haven't been enjoying a glass or two of nice Bordeaux. I mentioned earlier my parents were hippies who named me Om; to give you the complete picture they're still bohemians and these days live in a commune in rural northern Italy with my kid brother. My mum is French; my dad a Kentish man from Folkestone. As an only child, and somewhat older than mum, my dad has no living family left to speak of. My mum more than makes up for this deficiency; she grew up in the idyllic Normandy countryside on a farm along with her three siblings, all of them female; all of whom married and all who had children. In France there are many places Robyn and I can pick from to stay with my extended family when we frequently travel there.

Nanette is the only of my numerous cousins to be based in England. Five years younger than me, she's a solicitor for a French property company. A few months ago when they opened a London office, Nanette moved over from France to live in Chislehurst, South East London.

Nanette unexpectedly phoned one Monday afternoon in early January desperate for my kind of expertise "Om, I have the paranormal emergency going on here! I watch all of your videos from the first; I know you can help me. I have not slept for the three nights and this is getting too much for me! I cannot explain everything to you on the phone; can you and your most delectable Robyn come here to stay with me for a few days? I have my spare room ready for you; please do this for me cousin!" I had this call on speakerphone, I looked across at Robyn who nodded in the affirmative and mimed filming with her camera, after which I said "We'll be with you this evening Nanette. Do you mind if we film a paranormal case video in your apartment for my channel? We don't expect you to be it, we know as a professional woman you have a reputation to protect, we'll also not mention you by name". Nanette replied "Oui, I agree to all of that. I must say I am so relieved to know you are both coming here tonight, merci! And now I need to get back into court. À tout à l'heure!"

I mentioned my old van gets nervous in bad weather, in the gale force wind and pounding rain Robyn carefully drove us up to London that afternoon in her Fiat 500. Thankfully, as we arrived the storm seemed to have abated; we were in for quite the walk from where we were able to park to eventually arrive at Nanette's. The weather would remain reasonably calm for the rest of that night. Nanette didn't get back home from work that evening until 6.30pm; we arrived there thirty minutes after that time to ring on her intercom to finally see the apartment in question.

Robyn had not met Nanette before; she stared in shock at the woman stood before her. Nanette and I look like identical twins. I guess I should have mentioned this beforehand, but as I already knew this it didn't cross my mind it might look strange to Robyn!

Nanette stands as tall as me; and I am six foot one. We share the same hair and eye colour. Indistinguishable smiles, ditto with our facial expressions. We were born just one day apart, but with those five years between us. I guess we must look like some kind of weird male and female manifestation of the same person; well twins do I suppose, even when they're not genetic ones!

Having collectively hugged in greeting, Nanette said "Om and Robyn, as you know I have not lived here in England for so long, only a few months. You hear I am nowhere near as proficient at speaking the everyday English as I could be!" Robyn smiled at Nanette and said "Your everyday English is far superior to my everyday French Nanette. Are you two clones of one another?!" we laughed. I explained "Nanette is the eldest daughter of my mum's youngest sister, when she came along everyone thought it was us two who looked more like the siblings. As she grew up, well you can see for yourself! I am pleased you're only a short distance from us Nanette, we can see one another often" Nanette hugged me as she replied "For sure and I need to soon be coming to visit you both in Kent!" She would often do just that, but nothing paranormal ever occurred when she stayed with us in Kent, so it isn't worth relating here. Well, come to think about it though there was that one occasion by the River Thames up in London...but that's for later in the book.

Back in Nanette's place I got practical "What exactly are your paranormal problems Nanette? We want to help you if we can, please tell us all!" Nanette explained what had been happening "Oui, please do be helping me! I am totally creeped out in here! For the last three days the bathroom door started to be randomly opening all by itself, and I keep hearing the weird tapping noises when I am sadly all alone in my bed" Robyn looked across at me; we each knew exactly what the other of us thought, neither of us were picking-up on anything paranormal from around Nanette's apartment...

Robyn said "The best plan is for us to investigate when we have the place to ourselves" taking her cue, I asked "Will you be out at work tomorrow Nanette? What time do you usually leave in the morning?" she replied "I leave at half past seven and I am due in court for the morning, I think this is a simple building regulations legal contention to be finishing quickly, if thia is as I suspect I work only for the half day" Robyn concluded "This is perfect Nanette, tonight we shall observe and shortly after you have gone off to court tomorrow our investigation takes place!"

Nothing unusual or in the slightest paranormal occurred that night in Nanette's apartment. Robyn ordered in some Indian food and after finishing our evening meal, knowing we would all have early starts the following morning; we soon retired to our bedrooms.

In the privacy of our bedroom Robyn whispered "I am not getting the sense of anything psychic at all babe, how about you?" I whispered back "Nope Robyn, if there was some spirit here I am sure at least one of us would sense it". Robyn spoke her thoughts out loud "Ok, if this is not the work of a ghost, what might it all be about? What would cause the bathroom door to open by itself? And those weird tapping noises Nanette talks of, what could be causing them? When we get up first thing tomorrow soon we will discover why, what and how!" I kissed my wife, and by and by we eventually got some rest ready for the busy day ahead.

## EARLY START

Rising at before six the following morning, and staying as much as possible out of Nanette's way as she went about her usual routine of getting herself ready for work; Robyn and I also got everything ready for the shooting of our investigation video in her apartment. We enjoyed a coffee together before Nanette went off into her day. Looking at us Nanette suddenly proclaimed "Oh mon dieu, I had not noticed before! You are wearing wedding rings! When did that happen? And why was I not informed of this!?" she laughed as she said this part. Robyn replied "We went to stay in Glastonbury with an old school friend of Om's, this man officiated over a pagan handfasting betrothal ceremony for us as dawn broke over the horizon. He is ordained to also officiate at conventional weddings; he validated our marriage certificate and we left to return home officially married!" Nanette kissed Robyn's cheek and said "That is too romantic; there were just the two of you and this man?" I answered "We got a passing couple out walking their dog to witness the marriage, but essentially yes, we wanted this to be our own intimate and private ceremony". Nanette wiped a tear from her eye, and after looking down at her phone proclaimed "And now I really need to go off to the court! À tout à l'heure!" and with a slam of her front door she was gone to face the gale force wind of another stormy day.

With Nanette's apartment to ourselves we got down to business. Robyn set up one video camera on a tripod covering the main living area; the other she would carry. I carried with me our digital recorder for the sake of the film; although we already knew for sure this time we wouldn't be getting any EVP's.

Talking into the fixed camera sat in the living area I went through my setting-the-scene introduction "Greetings! I am Om Darke, and alongside me is the rather wonderful Robyn Humphries-Darke; yes viewers you heard that right; this is our first paranormal investigation case as a newly married couple! We're here in stormy London for our lockdown at Yvette's place. She doesn't want to appear on camera and we respect that. Yvette called us in as she's been unsettled by far too many weird experiences, Robyn will explain more" she took up the story "Yvette has been hearing unexplained strange tapping noises whilst she is trying to sleep. There is also a door we shall investigate shortly that Yvette has witnessed opening all by itself. She called us in to see if we might get to the bottom of these mysteries. If there is a spirit in this apartment we shall find it and deal with it for her"

Walking along the corridor away from the living area I said "This closed door here is the one Robyn mentioned. Yvette says this bathroom door opens by itself these last few days. She confirms this has only been happening recently, she's lived here for three months and up until this week nothing strange occurred. Robyn, I am not feeling anything at all paranormal here, how about you babe? Are you sensing any spirits here in this corridor or beyond in the bathroom?" Robyn responded "I am not getting anything at all babe! We shall need to find another explanation for this door opening in that spooky way!"

We filmed ourselves examining the closed bathroom door; it moved freely when we opened it. It honestly took us less than ten seconds to mentally solve this puzzle. We looked at one another and both proclaimed at precisely the same moment "It must be down to the wind causing this!" Anna Kostrová would be proud of our ESP and the synchronicity of our speech.

The conclusion we reached was off-camera. For the sake of our audience, Robyn went through the procedure of 'deducing' what the cause of the self-opening door phenomena could possibly be.

I took the role of camera man as Robyn talked "If there is no spirit acting as the cause of this door opening, there simply must be some more rational explanation. I shall leave this door slightly ajar and now conduct a small experiment. The toilet seat is down. I shall now lift it up. Om, please can you direct your camera at the door?" Sure enough it began to gently open, apparently all on its own. Robyn continued "These last four days we have all been experiencing gale force wind like I have never known before in England. With the toilet seat down nothing happens, lift the seat up and there is quite a draft coming from straight out of the bowl." Robyn pulled the bathroom door, but again not completely closed. She finished by concluding "Seat down and nothing. Seat up and we can watch as the door opens once more. This is nothing paranormal but all down to this ridiculously strong wind; when it eventually abates the issue shall go with it!"

We took a break to eat a late breakfast or perhaps it was more an early lunch; and enjoy another coffee. I said "We are one down, one more to go babe. That was brilliant the way you demonstrated the self-opening bathroom door, I know I could have stood there all day explaining away and not make it seem so simple!" Robyn answered "Merci Om and next we need to discover the root cause of this other non-paranormal mystery before Nanette returns!"

Robyn laughed as she added "This shall not be a ghost hunting video babe, more a case of watch the amateur engineers as they solve some engineery stuff!" I so love that woman! I replied "I don't think it matters there are no spirits to deal with this time Robyn, for sure there will be plenty of future cases where there are. If nothing else this investigation illustrates how we operate as a team on a complex case, and even without psychic phenomena, we go on to reach satisfactory conclusions as we solve everything for our client; plus we prove that debunking will occur on occasion".

Getting back to our case, we fell silent to listen. Speaking to Robyn's camera I whispered "We both hear a kind of gentle tapping noise coming from somewhere, but where exactly?" We wandered systematically through the whole apartment to gauge precisely where the tapping nose seemed to be at its loudest. Finding ourselves eventually stood outside Nanette's bedroom door.

At this point we cut filming and I texted Nanette, by now we knew her bedroom most hold the source of the noise; and we wanted her permission to proceed before filming in there and investigating further. Presently she texted back announcing that she had, as anticipated, finished in court and she would be returning home early in approximately two hours. She confirmed we could film in her bedroom, but asked Robyn and I to please tidy it for her first!

After a few minutes of putting Nanette's clothes back in the wardrobe, arranging her cosmetics and perfumes nicely on the dresser and moving discarded nightwear from off the bed, we resumed our filming.

I said into Robyn's camera "We've eliminated every other possibility Robyn, the source of the noise must be coming from behind Yvette's bedroom door". We opened the door and slowly made our way into the centre of the bedroom. In complete silence we stood there for a few moments, Robyn said "The noise is clearly coming from beyond the window babe; let's pull back the blinds to see where exactly"

We filmed the wild weather for some context to the video, showing everything outside getting blown around in the gale. Behind the block of apartments stood the paved yard area where strictly-only residents could park their cars; adjacent to this was an impressive large detached private house complete with extensive back garden. Robyn talked to her own camera "We have found the source of the weird tapping noise. Om, look at that greenhouse halfway down Yvette's neighbour's garden, see that apple tree getting bent over so far in this strong wind to be gently tapping on the roof of the greenhouse!"

Filming over, we both laughed at the absurdity of this case and kissed; we wondered if we had the time before Nanette arrived back and concluded that we probably didn't; and settled for more kissing. Nanette returned home in under half an hour and we gave her the good news about there being nothing paranormal in her apartment. First she looked shocked, as she started crying and laughing all at the same time in relief!

Nanette asked us to stay on for another night, informing us that as she would not be due in court until afternoon the following day, she could stay-up later. By way of thanks she offered to prepare us a plant-based meal with the two bags full of ingredients she carried in with her on her arrival home; she promised we would adore it.

Robyn quickly became assistant chef, realising Nanette knew her way around a kitchen far more proficiently than either of us did! She was highly impressed with Nanette's kitchen skills, she learned much from only observing her in action during that evening.

As the meal was cooking I took myself off to the vintners Nanette suggested which sat on the next block to her apartment. After braving the gale force wind that seemed determined to blow me into the road, I arrived at the shop in less than five minutes.

The man behind the counter looked up as I entered and then he did a kind of double-take. He said "Good Evening Sir and what can I get for you?" I replied "I would like three bottles of a good quality Bordeaux please" he looked even more spooked after I said this "Excuse me for asking you this Sir, but you wouldn't happen to be the twin brother of one of my regular customers would you? She is called Narette" I laughed

"We're first cousins, everyone says we look like twins, am I to take it she buys Bordeaux as well?" he smiled "It really is quite uncanny how alike you look; she never considers any other wine Sir" I replied "In that case three bottles of whatever she usually buys will be perfect!" I paid the man and headed back to Nanette's place.

Nanette served mushrooms in garlic sauce as the starter, followed by beefless bourguignon with vegan 'beef' rather than the meat and finished off with a fruit pie with vegan custard; all of which Nanette made entirely from scratch.

That evening the three of us feasted, talked less sense as the night went on, and laughed together right through until the early hours of the morning.

We surfaced at around nine o'clock the following day all feeling a little the worse for wear. After a late breakfast we hugged goodbye and left Nanette to head back home to the Kent coast. In the early days I was disappointed if one of my investigations didn't yield some kind of spirit or ghost; by this time in my life I was more philosophical. As Robyn drove us home we agreed that we were happy there wasn't anything ghostly to report on this case for Nanette's sake.

Robyn uses the surname Humphries-Darke. The name written on my own passport and driving license tells anyone who cares to read them my real full name is Om Humphries-Darke. I feel honoured to share my wife's surname alongside my own; but to make things simpler we agreed professionally I would carry on being just Om Darke; this is how I was already known to the millions of followers and subscribers on our channel.

Meanwhile, upon arrival back home, before having the time to even unpack our next case awaited us…

# 8
# ROMAN INVASION

"There are ghosts marching through our bedroom!"

The action here takes place straight after last chapter THE HAUNTED APARTMENT. As we walked through the door of our home, Robyn automatically turned-on her laptop she accidentally left behind in our haste to leave, to check for any possible future paranormal case contacts coming in from our video hosting message board. What immediately stood out to her was an email from a couple who contacted us while we were away; Bruce and Paula. They sounded rather desperate for our kind of help. Robyn emailed straight away asking when we might be able to meet. Paula came back immediately within a few seconds asking for us to please come and meet with them as quickly as we possibly could.

Robyn shouted upstairs "Babe, we find ourselves with a paranormal emergency from the tone of the emails; we need to leave for Canterbury within a few moments!"

After taking showers to freshen-up after the journey and getting changed, now the weather was dry once more I retrieved my old van from our garage and I drove us the short distance over to Canterbury.

In the freezing heart of winter the roads were pleasingly quiet, and we arrived at the couple's bungalow within two hours of Robyn and Paula exchanging emails. With Bruce out at work during the day, we'd be meeting with only Paula, who apparently worked from home. Robyn already asked if Paula minded us filming her talking about their haunting issue, to our delight she agreed this wouldn't be a problem.

We guessed Paula to be somewhere around thirty years old. She looked exactly like the artist she was, with large white framed glasses, her crazily curly blonde hair tied up with a white ribbon and cascading out of a messy bun, blue denim dungarees decorated with the paint from many works of art, her feet bare and with pink painted toenails. Robyn and I glanced at one another; Paula was so pretty and would look fantastic on-camera; making us all the more delighted she agreed to be interviewed. We set up our tripod and camera panning onto where Paula would sit, we'd already decided I would be the one asking the questions; Robyn's role was to act as camera woman filming me as I talked with Paula. We resolved that the photogenic Paula should remain the sole focus to the beginning of this case for the video, as she related to us her story. We'd film an introduction as part of the beginning of the interview;

and subsequently make our usual case video as we investigated and then all being well, closed the case for the couple.

I began "Greetings! I am Om Darke alongside me as usual is the wonderful Robyn Humphries-Darke my thoroughly incredible partner in life and paranormal investigations. We are in Canterbury with Paula. You tell us you are having an issue with a haunting, please explain exactly what you are experiencing Paula" she proved to be the perfect interviewee as Paula spoke solidly for the next five minutes without any further prompting "Mr Darke, it sounds as if we have soldiers marching straight through our bedroom as we try to sleep! Each night for weeks when Bruce, my husband, and I go to bed we can faintly hear the sound of multiple footsteps walking in step just like they're marching, and there are these murmuring voices just below the level where can properly make out what they're saying. Of course we tried recording these sounds on our phones but nothing could be heard when we listened back" Paula then fell silent. I asked "Can we come back here tonight Paula, around the time you usually settle down to try and sleep, and can we have your bedroom to ourselves for a while to allow us to thoroughly investigate?" with a smile of relief Paula responded "Yes, please do Mr Darke! Actually Bruce and l will go out to a neighbours for an hour then you've got the entire bungalow to yourselves!" I thanked her; and we left for now, until our promised return later that day.

We drove back home. Robyn said "We have many hours to wait before we need to return for the lockdown Om, I am going to take this opportunity for some research on the history of the area their bungalow stands. This might help us better understand the haunting" I thought of an idea "Robyn I am going to film you doing your research, and then you can discuss with me what you find for the video"

Robyn had a far better idea, off-camera she thoroughly researched the history of the area of Canterbury that Bruce and Paula's bungalow sat in. After having done all this and with multiple links ready on her laptop, for the sake of our video she then went through the process of 'finding' the information to tell me what she discovered on-camera.

Robyn talked directly into my camera "While we wait for our lockdown tonight I am online researching Bruce and Paula's bungalow. I see it was built in the mid-1980's. There is much history in this area; where it stands was once a public footpath. Perhaps this is not so interesting in itself. Yet my research reveals this path to have been an ancient right of way dating all the way back into history and the times when Romans occupied much of Britain!" I said "Robyn, as we know Canterbury has a well-documented history of Romans occupying the city from practically two thousand years ago. You mean to say this footpath really is that old?" She answered "Yes babe and some of this footpath still exists outside of the city? How about we go now and walk along this footpath to see if we encounter anything paranormal?" I responded "Sounds 1 a great plan Robyn, mon dieu it's bitterly cold today, for sure we'll need to wrap-up warm for this one!"

We placed our tripod and camera part of the way down this deserted footpath and walked slowly towards it; stopping a short distance from it for a conversation. As I anticipated it was a seriously cold winter's day, with temperatures well down in the minus degrees, although wearing our usually warm thermally insulated trekking coats, hats and gloves, we were still chilled through to the bone.

Robyn, who feels the cold more than I do, managed to say without her teeth chattering "Om, I feel paranormal activity here, are you also getting anything psychic coming through as we walk the length of this deserted two thousand year old right of way?" I responded "It's atmospheric here, we can both feel the history as we're walking and to answer your question Robyn, yes and very much so!" I looked around myself and added "This footpath is unbelievably active; all around me I sense multiple spirits." Robyn said "I believe we understand this case far better babe. We know now that we can help Bruce and Paula find some peace to finally be able to sleep in their home!"

We were as sure as we could be we knew exactly what the cause of the haunting was all about. We finished filming and went shopping for a few items to take along with us for our lockdown at the bungalow that night. As it was by now the early evening, rather than bother with going home and needing to return again, we went for an enjoyably leisurely meal at a favourite restaurant of ours in Canterbury.

As agreed, we arrived at the bungalow for 10pm, Paula introduced us to a tired looking Bruce, and then off they went to their neighbour's house for an hour as promised, leaving us to our lockdown.

We both held cameras, as we talked to one another "Robyn let's investigate the bedroom immediately. See if we also hear those same marching feet that are causing Bruce and Paula so many sleepless nights" she answered "On the floor by the window there is just about enough room for us to both fit, it's a good job we are a couple as we shall be up extremely close and personal!" I laughed, and we crouched down together in the confined space on the floor of the bedroom by the bed. We waited. Robyn whispered to my camera "Sure enough we hear the faint sound of multiple footsteps all around us and fainter murmuring voices. I am not sure the camera picks this up, nevertheless Om and I do hear them quite distinctly!" I confirmed "For sure Robyn, and it seems what we both intuitively thought would be the truth behind this haunting is right on the money" Robyn nodded in the affirmative and said "We must deal with this as we discussed babe, then Bruce and Paula can finally get that good night's sleep!"

I stood and took a beautiful clear faceted hanging crystal in the shape of sphere from out of my backpack to hang in the window. Robyn followed me with her camera, as I next placed a substantial piece of natural smokey quartz on the window ledge; walking from the bedroom another smaller piece of smokey quartz got placed on a small table used for keys positioned close by the front door.

Robyn spoke into my camera "The uncomfortable feeling in the bedroom has passed immediately. Babe, please explain what we deduced and why you placed those crystals as you did"

I spoke into Robyn's camera "The bungalow we stand in interrupted an ancient footpath when it was built. This path is actually a powerful ley-line in use for likely thousands of years. During Roman times centurions would have marched along here on their way to and from the Kent coast. They did this every single day for several hundreds of years, until they left Canterbury for good. Maybe some centurions died in battle right where we are standing in this bungalow? Naturally we'll never know for sure if this is true, but those footsteps we heard and which so disturb Paula and Bruce are from ghosts of these long-dead centurions. The quietly murmuring conversations are them talking; little wonder we couldn't decipher what they were saying!" Robyn asked "And what about the crystals babe?" I replied "The crystals I placed around the bungalow divert the leyline's energy around the building. They may of course be removed for cleaning, but absolutely must be sited back precisely where I originally placed them" Robyn concluded "We are both convinced we cured this issue, we shall wait to hear back from Bruce and Paula soon to know for sure"

The couple duly returned after their hour, we told them the history of the area and what we had done. They insisted on reimbursing us for all the crystals we placed around their home. Robyn asked if Paula could email early the next day after which we hoped to declare the case concluded.

Early the following morning Paula actually phoned Robyn instead "Hiya Robyn! We both slept like babies last night for the first time in months! All is quiet and we trust you when you say you have cured our home of the 'marching Romans' passing through our bedroom.

Thank you both so much!" Robyn couldn't hide her delight "Marvellous news Paula! Please keep in touch by email for the next few days then we can all be sure the issue is gone" and with that the case was closed.

# The Spirits at Jim's Bar

# 9

# COULD FLORENCE BE HEALED?

Anna Kostrová entered our lives once again…

Robyn decided to sell her pub. Every month without fail a major brewery made her an unsolicited offer to take Jim's off her hands. Robyn was pregnant; imminently becoming a mum became more important to her than owning Jim's. The next offer that got made for her bar, and inevitably this soon materialised, after some small negotiations, she accepted. Robyn walked away from the building that had been a central part of her life since she bought the place six years ago when aged twenty-five as a run-down pub and with her single minded vision turned it into Jim's Bar; named in honour of her late grandad, a man who adored pubs and with money she inherited from him financing the purchase. She gave up a promising teaching career to own Jim's. Robyn loved her time as resident pirate there, and eventually the less hands-on owner, but recognised this was the moment to let the place go.

Robyn saw it as the end of an era, but also the beginning of an exciting new adventure for all of us, especially our soon to make an appearance baby. We paid-off what remained of our tiny mortgage and Robyn bought a new Volkswagen Caravelle MPV as our family car. I came into the twenty-first century with a new Land Rover Defender to replace my old van; I wanted a car I knew our baby would be safe in when only the two of us travelled anywhere; a Land Rover seemed a good option.

## ANNA, ANNA AND FLORENCE

Anna Kostrová text messaged Robyn on Friday morning. As typical with Anna this contact came completely out the blue. She explained her mum was now also living in Kent, and would it be possible to drop in to see us both soon to ask us for a favour? Naturally Robyn texted back and told her that would be absolutely fine. Two minutes later she knocked on our front door!

Upon seeing Robyn she screamed and hugged her like she was her long-lost favourite sister "OMG Robyn, pregnancy looks so zpropadený good on you! See, I told you that you two needed to get married didn't I?" I grinned "I had no idea you were such a traditionalist Anna!" she turned her slightly mad gaze full upon me "Darke, I am and I'm not. I believe bringing children into the world is some serious business, that's why I never did. Don't you think two it's nicer you're married now your baby is on her way?" Robyn said "Her?" Anna replied "Oh, I guess you didn't want to know the sex of your baby, I'll bet you asked not to be told when they did the scans, yes?" Robyn responded with "Hmmm" Anna looked crestfallen "Sorry! Oh well, I might be wrong, hey?"

"Anna, what can we do for you" I asked, she glanced from Robyn to me and then looked Robyn straight in the eyes she said "I want to ask you to do a distant psychic healing for my mum" Robyn looked mystified "I am not a psychic healer Anna" she winked at Robyn "Yes you are Krásná. You might not know it yet, but you're an amazing healer!" Robyn took her seriously despite Anna's crazy grin and felt quite humbled by the complete trust placed in her; she asked "What precisely is this healing you are apparently convinced I can undertake all about?" Anna looked sad "My mum needs it Robyn, she's staying with me in Margate until she finds her own place" Robyn said "Really? I guess that it won't do any harm to see if I can help. Please tell me what the issue is Anna" who replied "She's been off her food, sleeps most the time and can't even be bothered to clean herself properly anymore". A shocked Robyn responded with her voice full of concern "Oh no Anna! I promise you that I shall give it my best shot at trying a distant healing for her!" Anna grinned as she replied "Thanks Krásná, I just know Florence will soon be feeling way better". After this last comment I re-joined the conversation "Anna, your mum is also called Anna. You were named after her!" Anna responded "Yes, I do know that Darke! Florence is her cat."

## ROBYN THE SHAWOMANIC HEALER

Anna eventually left and headed back home to Margate. Robyn looked at me and laughed "Oh my gosh babe! Is Anna really convinced that I can psychically heal her mum's cat? Do you think she genuinely believes I am latently this amazing healer?" I smiled at Robyn and answered "I must agree with Anna. When you do your meditation, straight after you come out of your trance focus on sending healing energy to Florence" Robyn looked doubtfully at me "You honestly believe I can do this babe?" I replied "Above all else this needs to be relaxed and never forced. Yes babe, I am as convinced as Anna is you can heal. You're a natural born Shamanic Healer" Robyn laughed and said "Shawomanic Healer, if you don't mind!" I am so in love with that woman!

Robyn being Robyn, naturally spent much of the rest of that evening researching psychic and shamanic healing on her laptop. She suddenly announced "The psychic healing of animals is definitely a specialist area babe. There are only a small handful of healers in the UK offering their services to those with ill pets. Having read of some of their cases I possess immense respect for them and certainly hold no desire to join their ranks! This shall be a one-off case for me babe; and only done as a favour for Anna and Anna, her mum"

Florence the cat was not especially old for a feline. Robyn doubted she could help and said as much to Anna, who assured her that both she and her mum certainly trusted she could and so would she please just get on with doing her healing thing for Florence!

After her morning meditation, as I suggested, Robyn attempted connecting to this cat and sending her healing energy. Once she got over the alien feeling of doing this, it became her daily routine for the next several days.

We arranged for Anna to pay us a visit again a week later for a progress report on Florence.

The following Friday, over dinner, Anna gave us an update on Florence the cat. Apparently she started to eat a little after only the second day of Robyn's treatment, and over the course of the week of her post meditation healings the cat in question gradually returned to pretty much her old self. Robyn told Anna "I have not the slightest clue how I might have healed Florence, or even if any of this was down to anything at all I did. She might have simply got better all on her own. I am not claiming personal credit for this healing in any practical way at all. Anna, please can I ask you to not share with anyone else that I treat pets; I only did it this just the once for you and your mum; I am aware now this is so terribly not my thing!"

Anna laughed and turned her slightly mad eyed stare full on Robyn and said "My Mum and I do know it's you who healed Florence and you're way too modest! I promise I won't mention how you helped Florence to anyone Krásná, your secret is safe with me" she winked and smiled warmly at Robyn; who looked from Anna to me and then back at Anna again, and laughed her soft gentle gift from the goddess laugh, shrugged her elegant shoulders "Thank you Anna. I think!" she finally said.

As a thank you, Anna senior sent us over a couple of bottles of nice Bordeaux along with her daughter. Robyn obviously wasn't drinking alcohol due to her pregnancy. Those two full bottles incredibly and magically turned into completely empty ones during an enjoyable evening of laughter spent with the mad as a box of frogs Anna. She used one of our guest bedrooms once again.

Anna arose early the following morning, we could hear the shower running in her en-suite bathroom and even more loudly her repeatedly signing Wannabe, the old Spice Girls hit, at the top of her voice complete with her strong accent. Robyn and I hugged good morning; and we couldn't help but laughing to the point where tears were streaming down our faces as we listened to our morning concert.

Twenty minutes later she knocked on our door, entering with a mug of steaming coffee for me and glass of cool water for Robyn. "Are you up for a chat?" we agreed we were. She sat on the end of our bed and began "Okay, here's the deal. How do you both feel about coming with me to for a week-long lockdown at a medieval castle up in Scotland hunting ghosts?" I confess this was all a bit left-field even for me! Rather ineloquently I responded "What?" Anna spoke as if talking to a toddler "I am asking if you two beauties fancy investigating the ghosts at a castle up in Scotland?" Robyn answered "I am busy being pregnant right now Anna! I cannot contemplate venturing out on any cases in my current condition" Anna laughed as she replied "You know I had already noticed your bump Krásná?" she continued "This possible case isn't until September next year" I said that in principal we would be interested. Anna beamed at us, her eyes positively ablaze with excitement "Oh that's zpropadený awesome guys! The Count wants to speak personally with you Darke; and then I reckon we're good to go on this!"

## WHO IS ANNA KOSTROVÁ?

Anna Kostrová was born in Prague in what is now known as Czechia but was then Czechoslovakia on the 13th November 1980.

Her mum unfortunately became a widow when Anna was only five; her husband died in a car accident on his way home from work one fateful day. This left Anna's mum, as we know she is also called Anna, as a single parent aged twenty three. She danced with a touring ballet company based in Prague, and when away her parents looked after little Anna. All the while she constantly looked for ways to build a better life for her daughter and herself.

Her ballet company toured England in 1988; and as part of this tour they were invited to perform in London alongside an English ballet company. Anna senior saw an opportunity to maybe switch ballet companies and countries to start a new life in England. Long story short, she got offered the opportunity to join this English ballet company, over half of which was already made up of non-native English dancers. They were based in London and she would join them in just three months' time. In the meantime she looked for a place for them both to live. Morden became her town of choice, not too far to commute by tube into London; it seemed like a good place to raise her Anna.

When they moved to Morden little Anna barely spoke any English, her mum was determined she would fit in and paid for her to receive both English and elocution lessons. By aged ten Anna spoke perfect English but never lost the strong Eastern European lilt to her accent. Anna senior stayed in England until her Anna went off to University to ostensibly study fashion; a course that she would abandon half way through to accept a job offer as junior fashion buyer at the London based head office of a famous department store chain.

With her ballet career reaching towards its end, in 2006 Anna senior returned to her native home country a rich woman through her years dancing. She set-up a hugely successful ballet academy in Prague, which she would sell upon her permanent return to England; although it still bears her name.

Anna had always been obsessed with the more extreme areas of the paranormal. Demonic hauntings fascinated her and long before she met me she had spent years venturing solo into some deeply disturbing places, more often than not without taking the trouble to get any official permission beforehand. We met when I got called in to investigate the building she worked in, and as the management were fully aware of Anna's unorthodox hobby, she got assigned to show me around. The rest as they say is history.

Anna is a maverick, always was and always will be. I honestly think she's far too full-on for most people to handle. I can't say I was exactly blissfully happy during those two years we spent together, as truthfully I wasn't. What we did do though was create some incredible case videos!

When she finally left I never regretted the time we spent together; I am eternally grateful though that she did go and I found Robyn. Anna and I would quite likely have met with some spectacularly gothic end consumed by some demons she provoked too far!

Robyn and I are for keeps; she is my wife, lover, best friend, soulmate and the reason I get up each day so that I get to spend more precious time with her. I get this might sound cheesy, but it's true.

Anna senior loves cats. When daughter Anna suggested she move back to England, one of the first things she did upon her arrival was take in a rescue cat. Anna senior had already been enthusiastically told all about Robyn and how she has this magic about her; she knew me well from my two years spent with her daughter. When Florence her cat fell ill she insisted Anna visit Robyn to ask for her help; and so we reach the point where she entered our lives again.

# 10

# A NOT SO EMPTY FACTORY

Robyn laughed her soft gentle gift from the goddess laugh as we spoke on the phone from the scene of the lockdown "I am hardly surprised that you would choose to investigate that place babe" she added more seriously "Although it's Nanette I feel for the most, it must have been too awful for her, bring her home with you!"

This wasn't any kind of an official case or commission from anyone wishing to discover more about the spirits haunting their building. This investigation came about because of my cousin Nanette.

She got in touch surprisingly offering us a paranormal investigation opportunity. Nanette told us about a client of her company who were soon to be demolishing this old factory building situated on the banks of the River Thames, intending to build luxury apartments in its place. She said she handled all the legal aspects of the various planning applications; and personally visited the potential development site to take photos, but only from outside. She told us she ended up in conversation with a local family who were walking their dog. These people confided in Nanette they were terrified of the building because of all the ghosts! Full of enthusiasm Nanette shared with us she had already contacted the contractor to ask for a key to the building, she didn't mention at this point he did warn her that she might not like to enter the building for what she would come face to face with, but she insisted and so he had a key sent one over to her by courier that same afternoon; she also didn't mention the hand-written note attached to the keys strongly suggesting she didn't use them!

She phoned us "Greetings Om, is Robyn there with you?" as usual I had put the call on speakerphone" Robyn answered "Hi Nanette, yes I am here "Nanette said "I have got the keys in my hand to the old disused factory overlooking the river in London; I thought you could investigate, but it must be tonight because the keys need to be returned tomorrow and I promised they would!" Robyn said "This one is going to be Cm doing a solo investigation this time, I am over eight months pregnant and feeling much alike the average barrage balloon!" Nanette laughed and made a suggestion "How about I come along with you on the investigation? I would very much like to see what you do when you are looking for the ghosts" this one came as a surprise. I said "Are you sure cousin? You do know this case will be filmed and put up on our channel?" Nanette replied "Oui, for sure I am sure Om" I looked over at Robyn for her opinion, who shrugged her elegant shoulders and said "Om shall be setting off to London in only a few minutes Nanette, picking you up on the way and heading to the site for early evening" and after our goodbyes, that's exactly what I did.

## THE INVESTIGATION BEGINS

I spoke into my own camera "Greetings, I am Om Darke. The rather wonderful and gorgeous Robyn Humphries-Darke is rather too pregnant to join me on this case, however I am not alone!" I panned my camera across onto my fellow investigator for this case "Allow me to introduce Nanette Fabienne, and before you ask, no Nanette is not my twin sister, but we are first cousins. Nanette, this lockdown came via you and your connections, tell us more about why we are here "Hello Om; oui this is most true. There are the local people being too scared to be visiting this portion of the river after dark because of all the ghosts!"

I continued speaking into my camera "Nanette's initiative has brought us to investigate this building behind us here on the banks of the iconic River Thames in London. This empty factory was once busy to the sound of workers, now it stands there eerily silent. Nanette and I will now begin our investigation to uncover what spirits are here!"

## THE INVESTIGATION ENDS!

It was the twilight of the evening when Nanette unlocked the door; as one we entered into the old factory building to immediately sprint straight back out again slamming the door behind us!

Nanette's deafening screams probably got heard right in the centre of London five miles away; she continued screaming for over ten minutes until eventually she began to loudly sob. She leant on me and I caught her as she fainted.

I carried her back to my car; it presented quite the challenge carrying a six foot one unconscious woman, who wasn't helping make this task any easier for me by flailing her arms all over the place. I somehow avoided her scratching my face like an angry cat with her nails and after what seemed like a walk forever carrying a seriously traumatised Amazonian woman, eventually I gently settled her into the passenger seat of my Land Rover. I took a few moments resting to get my breath back and phoned Robyn to tell her what had happened. Her response to our predicament opens this chapter; she saw the funny side from my perspective but obviously felt deeply for Nanette and insisted she shouldn't be left alone.

Nanette is severely musophobic, rodents utterly terrify her. When Nanette opened the door for us to enter;

hundreds of rats scattered; some of them running over our feet from out of the door and diving into the river. It would be several hours before Nanette could speak!

I didn't take her home to her own place, as Robyn insisted; I brought her back to Kent with me. Only after we had given her so much brandy for the shock she likely didn't even know her own name, she mumbled in French, which I translate for you "Rom and Obyn please don't ever take me home; I don't want to live in London anymore! Rom I love you; you're my best ever twin!" she passed-out after this, still wearing the same look of sheer terror written large upon her face. I carried her upstairs to bed; and left as Robyn undressed her and helped to settle her in.

The following morning through her hangover Nanette confessed all about the contractor's warning and the note he attached to the key he sent her. We arranged for a courier to collect the key from us and take it back up to London and then Nanette could keep her promise. With no court cases due for the next few days Nanette stayed on with us. Robyn stands five foot ten; she managed to find some clothes to lend Nanette she could just about squeeze herself into.

Nanette eventually went home and began the slow road to recovery from her nightmares, a month or so later Robyn made one of her regular phone calls to check how she was doing, after establishing she felt much better, Robyn said "Nanette please do not find us any more locations to investigate; we love you unconditionally and of course respect your considerable intelligence, however occasionally you behave so alike a stereotypical dumb blonde that it is too scary!" Nanette laughed at this one eventually answering "Oui Robyn...oui, I know this is true! I love you two, or now the three of you, so much as well! I promise I will not be finding any other of the buildings for you to be investigating. Perhaps I should be going chestnut like you to save myself?!" Robyn laughed and finished the call as Romy was quite insisting that her mum feed her.

# 11

# THE COUNT AND HIS CASTLE

"Allow me to introduce myself. I am officially known as the Earl of somewhere or other, which is all frightfully boring. Everyone calls me The Count…"

INVITES APLENTY

Anna had set-up her own video channel upon her return to England. I gave her copies of all the videos from our old cases to post on her channel, together with the one from the case of ours she more recently got involved with DEMON HUNTING AFTER MIDNIGHT. She also put up her own interview with Matt Iommi on her channel. I took a look; all her other posts were stream of consciousness vlogs; given the way her mind works Anna had amassed quite the number of subscribers who were doubtless fascinated to wait and see just what she might say next!

Personally we receive hundreds of invitations a year to investigate allegedly haunted houses, offices, factories and even caravans! We read them all, taking the time to personally reply to each one; usually to announce that regretfully we are fully booked-up and so cannot help on this occasion. If we feel it appropriate to the situation presented to us, we will make a few suggestions to the sender on how they might help themselves.

Out of a hundred contacts, there are perhaps around two percent that we email back with a few specific questions, depending upon their answers, we either agree we can talk further to discuss a possible case or if it doesn't feel quite right, then we don't.

After my non-investigation with Nanette in the factory by the River Thames, several cases had passed on by.

A client paid us well for our intervention to deal with his poltergeist; but as he was famously the drummer in a long established rock band he didn't want any publicity and no film got made; this case cannot be chronicled for the same reason.

Another case saw us heading over to the South West of England to investigate another multi-storey car park with a haunting issue, this time for a public limited company. This case did make it to video, but as the experience so closely parallels and mirrors earlier unfilmed case SUICIDE CAR PARK, it is too repetitious to share here.

There were more cases we also cannot share, to protect the privacy of our clients. Needless to say we were busy!

Romy mostly travelled with us on location; obviously if we thought there was any likelihood or chance there could be anything extreme we might encounter or the location could be hazardous, I went solo to investigate. We are of the opinion, clearly within reason, children need to be integrated into and included within the lives of their parents. In our case this meant Romy travelling with us on paranormal investigations; she happily slept through most of these!

Anna passingly mentioned to us late the previous year a possible case involving a week long investigation up in Scotland at a medieval castle for some character known only as The Count. As we hadn't heard from her since; we gave no further thought to the matter.

Typically unannounced, Anna Kostrová knocked on our front door one day in late May.

ANNA MAKES A CONFESSION AND A PROPOSAL

Robyn answered the door with Romy in her arms, Anna grinned like she'd just realised she held the winning ticket to the lottery. In an unbelievably gentle quiet voice for her, Anna said "Krásná, it's so great to see you! And who have we here? She is adorable! What's her name?" Robyn replied "Anna meet Romy!" Anna thought for a moment "I get it; Romy is both your names combined, yes?" Robyn smiled "Yes Anna; would you like to hold Romy after you have washed your hands?" Anna actually giggled, I mean really! I watched this from the kitchen and can personally attest that Ms Demon-Hunting-Goth-Queen herself did genuinely giggle. She looked wide eyed at Robyn "Can I really? Oh yes please! I'm off to scrub my hands like I'm about to perform surgery. Hiya Darke, you and Krásná make the cutest babies ever!" she said this last part to me as she passed on her way to the downstairs washroom.

Emerging over fifteen minutes later Anna smelled like an advert for anti-bacterial hand wash. We all sat on the sofa and Robyn handed Romy over to her. She became quite overcome with emotion; she asked Robyn if it was okay to hug Romy, after getting permission she ever so gently hugged her to herself "Oh I adore the smell of babies! Honestly Romy is the most beautiful baby I ever saw in my life, I don't just say that, she is for a fact! Look at you miláček with all your perfect little fingers and toes. I'll hand Romy back to you now Krásná because next I'm going to cry for a while!" and she did exactly that as well. We didn't know quite how to react to this, Anna waved away both of our offers of a hug, so we just let her cry until she was done.

Once she seemed calmer, I asked "Why are you here Anna? There's usually a reason for you knocking on our front door" I smiled at her as I said this to show her I wasn't being mean.

Anna dried her eyes and oddly didn't bother rushing off to sort out her make-up out; eyeliner streaks went from her eyes practically right down her neck and she didn't seem to care. "I've got a confession to make to you both" we waited for it "You might remember that last time I was here I mentioned a certain possible case up in Scotland?" we nodded in the affirmative "Well, this all came through my video channel from one of my followers. He'd seen our old case videos Darke, and then the later one with the all of us and assumed the three of us must be a team. He got in touch suggesting this week-long lockdown at his castle. Okay, I admit I got a bit carried away and agreed; but he wants to talk to you first Darke. I printed out his message so you could both read it.

*Dear Anna, Robyn and Mr Darke,*

*Allow me to introduce myself. I am officially known as the Earl of somewhere or other, everyone calls me The Count. I am linking my website here so you know I am for real.*

*I would like to cordially invite you all to stay for a whole week as my personal guests here at my castle. Some ghosts asked for you by name to meet them for a pow wow, and you can't really let poor lonely ghosts go un-pow wowed can you?*

*I want you to tell me all about my ghosts'*

*What say you, good people? Mr Darke please give me a jolly old phone call to discuss all the boring stuff like when from and until; and how many sacks of money I can give you.*

*Yours etc,.*

THE COUNT

Anna continued "I agreed in theory for us to start our lockdown beginning on the week 5th September. All it needs now is for you to talk to him Darke!"

Robyn and I looked at one another in the eyes for a few moments, after which I said "Yes Anna; Robyn and I agree in principal to all of this. We have nothing else on that week. This will require some detailed planning, but we're for sure up for this one Anna. We agree that firstly I talk to this Count to see if it all seems above board and feels right, after we can see from there together how to make this all work."

Anna looked from one to the other of us with her slightly mad stare and then at Romy who was now asleep; ever so quietly she asked "You decided all that just from looking at each other like that for a minute? OMG you two are so soulmates, that was incredible! Krásná, tell me honestly, is that what you were really thinking when you looked at your husband?" she replied "Yes it is Anna. To the last full stop, crossed T and dotted I! That is honestly exactly how I wished him to convey to you our commitment to this case" Anna gently sighed "Oh _____ wow!"

## A JOLLY OLD PHONE CALL

"Good morning, may I speak with The Count please?" I asked "No need to introduce yourself, I know exactly who you are. I am utterly delighted you phoned me Mr Darke and a jolly good morning to you!" The Count replied.

I don't surprise too easily, yet for a brief moment I found myself rather lost for words, I quickly recovered my composure "I suppose you recognise my voice from the videos, yes?" The Count replied "Sadly I'm not psychic like all of you; I don't know if you are aware what a distinctive voice you possess Mr Darke? And I did request that you give me a jolly old phone call, I know the head honcho when I see one!" He continued with "Mr Darke, how do you and your two outstandingly stunning colleagues fancy visiting this little squat of mine, spending a week of abject debauchery and vampirism with me; oops sorry, naughty Count! I rather meant would you care to toddle along here for seven days to say bonjour or in alluring Anna's case ahoj to my ghosts; you'll enjoy scoffing my vegan food, chef seems to know what he's doing; and drinking oceans of superb vintage wine from my cellar!"

I responded "Count, we make our decisions collectively and we all need to be in agreement before we take on any case; there is no head honcho as you suggest. As I have been doing this the longest, I act as team-leader on our lockdowns, and that's all. We have already talked between us, subject to ironing out a few details; we would like to accept your offer of the week long stay, erm minus any of the debauchery and vampirism!" The Count laughed, I continued "As Anna told you, we do have a full week with no other commitments beginning the 5th of September. Does that work for you Count?"

The Count said "September is quite fine by me Mr Darke, 'it rocks' to use the modern vernacular; there is nothing else booked in at the castle that week, you shall have free run of my entire little squat! Oops, there's an elephant in the room with me asking how many sacks of money I can give you!"

I explained "We like to be upfront with all the costs then there can be no misunderstandings later. Our latest case lasted four hours for which we were paid five thousand pounds, plus our travel expenses and hotel costs, as the fee for our time. I know our client won't mind me telling you this; they're a PLC so this is all a matter of public record anyway. Please suggest a figure to me Count and we can see how far apart we might be"

The Count pondered for a moment "Well, I am sure you will have thoroughly researched me and know from my website we host wedding events at the castle. I mean obviously this is nothing to do with me personally, I employ the services of an excellent wedding planner to organise them. Typically for a wedding we charge 20k for the day. How does 100k for the week sound to you Mr Darke or am I insulting you and you'll never speak to me again?"

"120k and we have a deal" I admit I chose this amount at random; after all we ended up achieving over that week and some of the decisions we needed to make, I feel like I ended up underselling ourselves and frankly should have insisted upon twice that amount when we were negotiating. Live and learn, as they say.

"Oh how marvellous! The elephant is ecstatic we sorted that one out. Mr Darke, I have the lovely photographer itching to take some snaps of you arriving and toddling around my little squat meeting Bert and all the rest of my ghosts, apparently they'll look 'awesome' up on our social media pages; if that's all hunky dory with you? Say you agree and I'll personally cook you a vegan dinner myself!" I couldn't help but laugh, The Count really was something else "Yes, of course, if you please let me have digital copies of all these photos for our own social media?" The Count responded "Deal! My word, aren't we getting along well? Next we must get onto some tiresome practicalities! We have ten decadent hotel rooms in the castle, should wedding guests wish to stay over for a night or two and of course, if they possess deep enough pockets. If it's okay with you Mr Darke, three of these hovels shall be yours for the week"

"These are double rooms, yes?" The Count replied "Yes Mr Darke, all of them are" I said "We'll only be needing two rooms Count; Robyn and I are married with a seven month old baby" The Count laughed "Of course! I should have realised. I remember thinking back about it now; you and Robyn did keep calling one another 'babe' when you were chasing that demon around Kent. How totally hilarious I hadn't put two and two together!" The Count laughed again; after a moment or two's thought he added "You say you have a seven month old baby?" I confirmed we did and told him her name "What are you going to do with Romy while you're busy investigating my ghosts? Is there anyone you trust enough to baby mind for you" I looked across the room at Robyn who'd been listening to the entire call on speakerphone and got immediately who she meant when she mimed banging down a gavel "My cousin Nanette Fabienne is about the only person in the World we would trust with Romy in all honesty Count" he enthused "I insist she come along with you to stay here as well and become part of our exploration into debauchery and vampirism; oops, of course I mean your lovely paranormal investigation. We shall go back to our deal of the three rooms Mr Darke. Nanette must treat it like a holiday; she simply must come up here with you to the castle and relax for the whole week!" I replied "Nanette works as a property lawyer in London, I know she hasn't had any holiday this year. I think she will be up for your suggestion Count" The Count misses nothing "She is a property lawyer? I happen to need the services of just such an expert, synchronicity is wonderful isn't it? I shall try not to bother Nanette on her holiday and yet having her on hand is too good an opportunity to pass on by!" I replied on her behalf "She works for a French property company, she's based in their London office, I know she won't mind having a chat with you about property law, but she might not be legally able to offer you any advice" The Count came back with "Sounds fair enough" and with that all said, apart from our respective goodbyes, the jolly old phone call was over.

Robyn laughed her soft gentle gift from the goddess laugh "Oh my gosh what a character The Count is! I am so proud of you babe, you handled that beautifully. Romy is sound asleep, why don't we re-enact how we made her?" we did just that for the rest of the afternoon.

JOURNEY TO THE CENTRE OF THE CASTLE

September came around quickly. I said "We're under one hour away from the castle; we'll stop here for coffee, and to freshen Romy and ourselves up. It's already mid-afternoon. I'll text The Count to inform him we are to be arriving soon. The lovely photographer, as The Count called him, will be waiting for us"

Back in the car we sat ourselves in the seats everyone had chosen eight hours earlier when we set off from Kent. Anna and Nanette stayed over with us the night before, and then we could get a nice early start in the morning. Upon meeting Nanette, Anna had of course made her expected offer to share a bedroom with her; and yet knowing her well there was the sense of her kind of going through the motions of saying what was expected of her with no real feeling or emotion, her heart just didn't seem to be into flirting. Most impactful of all was Anna's new look. Gone were her usual hardly there black dresses and signature heavy gothic eye make-up; in their place Anna wore a slightly above the knee red kilt and white shirt; her face devoid of any make-up at all and her blonde hair grown out long past the bob she'd worn for as long as I'd known her.

Nanette sat in the front next me; I was happily doing all the driving. Although there are three seats up front in our Caravelle, Anna chose to sit in the second row of seats with Romy in her car-seat between her and Robyn. I'd removed the third row of seats to fit all our luggage, Romy's stuff and our investigation paraphernalia into the car.

Upon arrival, I parked near the entrance on the deserted public car park next to the castle, we got Romy into her pushchair, unloaded our wheeled cases and also wheeled equipment boxes; following arrows directing us which way to go, we passed through an archway, and across a vast courtyard to finally arrive at a substantial oak door with reception written on a brass plaque affixed to it.

A tall man with a large camera sprinted from out of a door on the far right hand side of the courtyard "You must all be The Count's VIP guests, phew I nearly missed you!" he gasped "Before you knock on the door, The Count wants a photo of you all arriving, if that's okay?" Robyn replied "We shall wheel all our stuff over there out of shot, and stand on these steps to pose prettily for you. How do you want us?"

The lovely photographer said "Thanks. Please stand on the bottom step framed by the door. Oh wow! You look uber cool in that kilt! Beautiful! Everyone else you are also nicely photogenic; makes my job all too easy. You should see some of the wedding guests I need to try and make look good! I'll be leaving you to it; you will be seeing me again from time to time. Thanks again!" and with that he was gone as quickly as he arrived.

A concerned Nanette said "I am not the part of this case or investigation! I ought to have stepped away when he was taking his photo so he captured only the three of you involved" Robyn reassured her "You needed to be in the photograph Nanette, Romy isn't a part of the investigation either and yet she is also in it! You are our token French woman; and of course every paranormal team legally requires one of those!" Nanette laughed at this. Anna said "I understand why he gets called 'the lovely photographer'; he's exceptionally lovely isn't he?" I teased "You're saying that because you're the only one of us he appeared to notice! At least he conceded we're also a bit photogenic, but nothing at all like his beautiful Anna!" we all laughed, I continued with teasing "The lovely photographer only has eyes for Anna-of-the-kilt!" who responded by pretending to smile dreamily as she said "I cannot deny it, I enjoyed all of his attention and especially the compliments!" we all laughed again.

The door behind us slowly began to open seemingly of its own accord, quite clearly there was nobody behind it, and yet it now stood fully wide open before us!

Robyn was the first to speak "I believe we are meant to go in" we found ourselves entirely on our own in a room that was some kind of weird hybrid between a grand castle and hotel reception. We walked on thick carpet, all around us on the stone walls hung tapestries alongside various swords and other gruesome looking weapons. To our left, through an archway we saw a larger room filled with white wooden chairs and a raised platform directly in front of them, the room was dominated by a resplendent grand staircase. As the modern reception desk sat directly in front of us sat empty; we left our luggage in front of it and made our way through into this other room. A high ceiling with vast light-fittings illuminated us, the floor was flagged grey stone, and more tapestries and weapons hung on the walls. Nanette said "Look at all the tapestries, how old must they be?" A loud voice came from behind her "All fake I'm afraid darling, yet they do add that certain je ne sais quoi our wedding guests seem to expect. Welcome to you all! I am The Count and this is my humble little squat" He stood halfway down the grand staircase, raising his arms above his head he gestured all around him pivoting on his feet. He walked down to meet us.

We already knew that The Count was forty years old from his personal profile on the castle website, yet nothing could possibly prepare anyone for coming face to face with him for the first time…

There is no other way of saying it; the man looked like a vampire! The Count was of slim build, with prominent cheekbones and stood the same height as Nanette and I, with dark hair swept back off his high forehead, his pale complexion made his sapphire blue eyes seem even more dramatic. He was dressed in a deep purple velvet jacket and waistcoat, tight black trousers, he wore a white shirt with black bow-tie, and of course he had matching black boots. The Count carried a black silver topped cane; we would soon learn he used this to point out things around his 'little squat' he wished us to observe. Robyn smiled inwardly to herself thinking he looked exactly like he had stepped straight out of one of the classic vintage horror movies they showed late night on Fridays on television when she was a teenager and that scared her so much she couldn't sleep; but she still had to watch again next week!

"Mr Darke, I am delighted to make your acquaintance, we can compare fashion later!" I replied "It is, erm nice to meet you Count, allow me to introduce…" this was as far as I got. "Ravishing Robyn I am most delighted to meet you, and you must be Romy!" He kissed Robyn's hand and waved at Romy who giggled at him "It's not often my little squat is blessed with the presence of three angels sent from heaven for me to enjoy, it seems today fortune decided to bless me" he took in Anna "Oh my, aren't you a sight for sore eyes in your wee kilt? I may well have to take to my bed after witnessing your attributes so wonderfully on display; if you would care to join me then my year is made!" Romy giggled again, clearly she found The Count a very funny man, I wished I shared her enthusiasm for his sense of humour! He reached Nanette next "Nanette is looking all prim and proper in her business suit; be still my beating heart! What's that perfume you're wearing darling, it's driving me wild with unbridled lust or perhaps that's you?"

Nanette is a lawyer and quite used to thinking on her feet in court arguing her case, she wasn't in the slightest bit phased by The Count "Darling Count, is that the pistol in your pocket or are you just pleased to be seeing me?" to this The Count delightedly responded "The incomparable Mae West! Marry me this instant Darling Nanette, I insist we name our first-born Mae in honour of this moment, he won't be pleased!" Nanette instantly came back with "Marriage is the great institution, but I am not ready for an institution" The Count threw his head back and laughed "Darling Nanette you're a jolly old film buff!" she replied "I am not jolly old monsieur, I am but twenty nine!" I'd never seen Nanette in action in court, if this was an example of how she took down her adversaries it's no wonder her company paid her expenses to move from Paris to London! She carried on "Admittedly though Darling Count, I am the complete nerd for old movies" The Count asked her "Would you care to watch The African Queen with me on my overbed projector Darling Nanette, sadly it often breaks down and we might need to find other ways to amuse ourselves!" Nanette responded "Darling Count, I would immediately jump into any of the beds with you for the promise of an evening spent with Humphrey Bogart!" He grinned at Nanette, bowing to her in appreciation at her bantering skills; and then turned his attention back to us "My jolly old pater passed away when I was only twenty five from too much high living; he fell off his tightrope and died!" Romy giggled delightedly and we all groaned at this bad taste humour. The Count grinned at our reaction "Okay, truthfully the third heart attack saw him off when he was fifty. I've been the Earl of wherever since. I pay scant attention to my title. 'The Count' came from my time at Eton and references my vampiric appearance rather than anything hereditary!"

"I'll show you to your rooms, you must all be exhausted after your long journey!" The Count pointed his cane in the direction of the archway back into the reception area, and off he strode with four adults and one baby in his wake. Behind the reception desk to the right stood a door, The Count opened this revealing a substantial lift with more than enough room for the five of us, him and our entire luggage. As the lift slowly began to move Robyn said "The front door is automatically opening, until our photo was taken it was unpowered, you watched us on the CCTV to switch it back on when he was finished with us for the drama of the door opening by itself!" The Count exclaimed "Ravishing Robyn, you should teach engineering if you ever decide to quit being a ghost hunter; I promise you I would attend all of your lectures! And next, before we reach your rooms, let's detour in here for a moment to meet Bert!"

With a flourish The Count flung open a door on his right revealing a substantial room. "To our wedding guests this is known as the 'The Ballroom' which they seem delighted to accept at face value. Who knows it maybe even got used the once back in the mists of time for this purpose. Bert is waiting over here, come and say hello!" He pointed with his cane to a substantial stone fireplace, in fact large and high enough we all could have stood underneath it should we have wished to. The Count explained "The story goes that one of my illustrious ancestors in mid-Victorian times employed the services of a jolly old chimney sweep. He scarpered up and back down every chimney in the place until he came to this one; with a cheery smile clearly visible on his sooty face off he went to explore the darker recesses of this dinky little chimney; all seemed fine and dandy until with a horrible scream poor old Bert rapidly descended head-first straight back down to crash into that very grate right there!" He pointed with his cane. We all observed the scene of the accident.

Robyn said "We don't really think his name was Bert do we Count? There is the infamous 'Cockney' character in a certain movie musical known as Bert The Chimney Sweep" The Count winked at Robyn "You are of course quite correct" I'd remained silent since leaving the main hall, now I said "He's a restless spirit who doesn't know he's dead. I strongly feel his presence" Anna added "He used foot and hand holds inside the chimney; missed one of them in the darkness and fell. Count we'll return to this room to investigate in the morning, between us I'm sure we can unravel the mystery of who Bert really was" Robyn said "We shall see if he can communicate through our devices and learn as much as we practically can about him for you!" The Count responded "Splendid! As promised, I'll now show you to your rooms, shortly after dinner shall be served. By the way, there's no need to dress for dinner. Come however you please, in fact why bother dressing at all you ladies? I promise I shan't be shocked!"

Our three rooms all stood adjacent. They were akin to the best boutique hotel, resplendent with modern four poster beds and white plastered walls, unlike all the other rooms in the castle.

After a delicious meal, exhausted after our journey, all five of us retired early to bed and almost instant sleep.

# The Spirits at Jim's Bar

# 12

# BERTIE MACDONALD

Still in their respective nightwear, everyone converged on our room for a planning meeting on how best to proceed with the investigation early the next morning. Robyn began "We investigate 'Bert' today, who I fully researched on my laptop after dinner to find nothing further on him that The Count did not already tell us" Anna proclaimed "Nanette you were amazing yesterday, I didn't get the chance to talk with you about it after, but you went for it girl; I don't think The Count expected that!" Nanette laughed "Slightly off the topic Anna! I encounter many of the men in my profession who adore bantering with me in court. I do confess I thoroughly enjoyed myself, I adore some of the harmless banter!" I said "The Count did mention wanting to talk to you about property law Nanette, I assured him you would listen, but you likely couldn't offer any advice" Nanette said "Oui, you are most correct cousin. I find him later today to see what this is all about"

The Count announced during the previous evening's dinner he would be incommunicado out on his estate for most of the following morning into mid-afternoon; but encouraged exploration wherever we wanted in his absence "Treat my little squat as your home; go hither and thither as the mood takes you! All of my staff knows to keep well out of your way; although the lovely photographer will toddle along to catch a few snaps of you in action in 'The Ballroom' with Bert"

Our equipment tally had grown since the early days: Three professional lightweight hand-held video cameras; four fixed video cameras mounted on tripods which we placed around locations to capture any anomalies; digital recorders and walkie talkies. Co-ordinating all this wasn't usually such an issue, we generally left the fixed cameras to do their own thing and watched back later to analyse for anything interesting we may have captured, to which I recorded a voiceover.

Filming there at the castle was different. We would collectively record many hundreds of hours' worth of video by the end; if anything exciting showed up on a fixed camera we needed to be able to head straight across to the scene to investigate right there and then. A control room or hub was essential; and vitally someone placed in there we trusted to monitor everything, and inform us immediately if we needed to converge on an anomaly.

Nanette volunteered "I would be most delighted to fill the vacancy as your extra pair of eyes! Romy can be here with me in control. I link all your fixed cameras onto my laptop on split-screen the four ways, that way I cast the eyes on all of them simultaneously; I keep the guidebook with the map of the castle there in front of me, then I know precisely where to send you as promptly as the possible if anything shows up and I walkie you"

Robyn thanked her "It is all decided then. Thank you Nanette, it is reassuring to know you are the one having our backs. We shall work alongside one another setting up the hub in the area behind the reception desk. The Count assured us this is the most central location for our base of operations and he said leaving our equipment there is safe as the main door is dead-locked"

Nanette replied "I am au fait with computers, however you are far more of the expert than me Robyn, guidance in getting everything up and running smoothly would be most fantastic!" Robyn smiled genially "We shall be streaming onto both mine and your laptops, this is more efficient then you only need the one split screen on each so you easily see more" Nanette laughed looking over at Anna and me "See what I am meaning?!"

When we arrived at our morning rendezvous outside the door of 'The Ballroom' Anna wore a floral maxi-dress and sandals, no make-up and her hair up in a ponytail. I said "Anna we need to talk" Asking Robyn if she would mind setting everything up on her own, I took Anna over to the other side of the room and asked her if she had any problems she wanted to discuss. At first she assured me everything was good; then she looked me straight in the eyes and confessed all "I desperately want what you two have Darke! Please believe me when I say I'm not jealous of you and Robyn; I love Romy so much Darke and watching your two's connection in action causes me goose bumps. I'm forty one in two months Darke; it's still not too late for me to have a family with the right man. I don't want to be a scary woman anymore or go kicking the ass of demons! I just want a nice man I love and who loves me, a home to call our own and a family!" Robyn could hardly have failed to hear all of this, Anna isn't really known for her quiet voice, she came over to us and hugged Anna, who smiled at her. Robyn and I looked at one another; the slightly mad look was gone from Anna's eyes. Robyn said "You know what? I love this new you Anna!" and they hugged again.

We needed to begin our lockdown. Robyn had set-up fixed camera's one and two covered the fireplace from directly in front and from the side respectively. She'd already turned them both on and their link back to the hub sometime before and so we got underway.

I spoke into Robyn's hand-held camera "Greetings! This is Om Darke, with me as usual is the rather wonderful Robyn Humphries-Darke; joining us for the next few lockdowns I am delighted to announce the return of the incomparable, the one, the only, Anna Kostrová!" I didn't describe her as our demonologist anymore; it didn't feel right "Today finds us out on location in atmospheric Scotland investigating a tragic death and mysterious haunting at a medieval castle. This video is the first of three brand new lockdown specials coming up, based right here at the castle. Anna, explain we are investigating this particular room" talking into my camera she said "The fireplace behind me was the scene of a tragic accident one hundred and fifty years ago. Events on that awful day left their impressions deep in the walls which we can all feel. Robyn, what are our objectives today?" Robyn also looked into my camera "The owner of this incredible castle invited us for a week long investigation; this room is the highest priority for him and so this is where we begin. Only legends and myths surround the man who died in this very room, the owner asks us to please discover as much information about him as possible. Our mission on this lockdown is to find out all we can about the man they call Bert!"

Robyn's walkie sprang into life "Nanette to Robyn come in, over" Robyn replied "Robyn here, what have you seen Nanette, over?" she replied "As you were all talking; on fixed camera two I see the light anomaly; an orb travelling from the ceiling went down through the floor about one metre behind Anna, over" Robyn responded "Good spot Nanette! Over and out!"

Robyn said into my camera "There is paranormal activity already! Nanette Fabienne is back in our central hub, she is our vital extra pair of eyes this week, she has just seen an orb behind Anna and we caught it on our fixed camera two! We play this footage for you now, so you see for yourselves"

Cueing in video footage captured on a fixed camera with a voiceover is my province; Robyn took the initiative live this once as she knew for sure the orb film in question would be played at that exact moment because in the edit I would slot it in!

Anna and Robyn walked over to the fireplace for a quiet off-camera conversation. Robyn's walkie sprang into life again and this time I picked it up "Nanette to Robyn, over" I came back with "It's me here Nanette, over" she said "The lovely photographer, he is sat with me, he wants to know if he can come up to your location, over" I glanced across at Anna and Robyn who nodded in the affirmative "Please send him straight up Nanette, thank you, over and out".

Anna called across the room to me "We were actually just saying we wondered when the lovely photographer would turn-up, we don't feel we're able to get properly started under the constant threat of being disturbed; once he's gone we'll commence our lockdown proper by bolting the door from inside. Robyn and I have a plan we've wanted to try for ages, we were only waiting for the right opportunity, and this plan might just get us spectacular results!"

"Good morning ladies and gentleman! Are you okay with me calling you ladies or would you prefer 'women' 'girls' 'people' 'them'?" Robyn answered him "Ladies is fine, it is how we collectively refer to ourselves. What do you wish us to be doing whilst you take the photo?" He replied "How about you are all over by the fireplace? Please pose like you are in the middle of whatever it is you do on a ghost hunt; don't look directly at me" I took hold of a digital recorder and joined Anna and Robyn by the fireplace; Anna closed her eyes, I held out the turned-off digital recorder in front of me, Robyn stood with a camera 'filming' us. "That is amazing ladies and gent! Now please move to stand in a circle like you are having a discussion. You are naturals at this! Nearly done" We stood in a circle, as requested. "That's it ladies and gent, I am done! Thank you so much. Where are you going to be tomorrow? The tall French lady with the cute baby in your hub wasn't too sure" Anna replied "Hi, I'm called Anna" he smiled at her "Hi Anna, so pleased to properly meet you!" she smiled back "You too miláček!" she continued "We're investigating outside at the castle ramparts tomorrow, when hopefully it won't be raining like it is today! Although this castle proved impenetrable, this didn't stop potential invaders from trying to gain access, we want to see if we can make contact with any of them" he said "Cool Anna, if that's the case I likely won't need to disturb you, I shall get some shots of you from the turrets looking down, you won't even know I am there! Thanks again ladies and gent" we collectively said "Bye" and off he went, after which I bolted the door from inside. Anna remarked "The lovely photographer, he's just too cute!" we politely agreed with her.

After the door was bolted, Anna picked up her camera and focused on Robyn who said "We shall try the plan we talked about Anna; this is something new to both of us and not without risk. Babe, I am afraid your role in this is solely to film us; we shall neither of us be able to use cameras. This is going to either work spectacularly for us Anna or we fail miserably!" Anna calmly replied into my camera "It's okay Robyn, we can always opt to go back to our conventional methods if we crash and burn on this; yet you know Krásná, I've got the feeling this is really going to work!"

I followed them with my camera as they walked into the fireplace together. Anna and Robyn hugged one another tightly with their heads held closely together, both of them now stood directly under the middle of the opening for the chimney. I now knew what they were about to attempt and I admit my heart leapt into my mouth at the prospect!

Speaking over Anna's shoulder, Robyn explained all into my camera "Anna and I are attempting to join together to combine our psychic powers. This is something we have never tried before, which is particularly dangerous for Anna! We trust one another implicitly; there is no way we would ever contemplate doing this if we did not. If this works out as we anticipate it ought, Anna forms our direct psychic connection to this spirit and then I may ask her questions; if everything goes according to how we plan she can provide us with direct answers about the mystery of Bert"

Anna and Robyn fell silent, all that could be heard was the sound of the two psychic's rhythmic breathing as it became synchronized together as one, and there in the background rain gently pattering against the windows.

Eventually, after a considerable wait of practically one full hour…

Robyn - Are you here with us?

Anna talks in a broad Scottish accent – Aye lassie!

Robyn – What year is it?

Anna – Ye dinnae ken? It's 1867 lassie!

Robyn – What is your job?

Anna – Can ye noo tell?

Robyn – You are a chimney sweep.

Anna – Aye, that I am.

Robyn – What is your name?

Anna – MacDonald's mae name. Ye a Sassenach lassie?

Robyn – Frenchie, Mr MacDonald. What is your first name?

Anna – Bertie. Ah dinnae ken ye Frenchie. Whit's yer name?

Robyn – My name is Robina.

Anna – Aye? Hoo are ye Robina?

Robyn – I am very well. How old are you Bertie?

Anna – Dinnae ken Robina. Dinnae ken.

Robyn – Do you have family Bertie?

Anna – Aye. Two wee bairns Robina.

Robyn – And a wife Bertie?

Anna – Aye that I ave! Yon bonnie lassie like ye Robina!

Robyn – Thank You. Do you live close to here Bertie?

Anna – Aye Robina, it's noo so far.

Robyn – Did you fall ever fall in a chimney?

Anna – Dinnae ask mi that! Yon bad luck Robina!

Robyn – Sorry Bertie, I didn't mean to upset you.

As no other information came through Anna and Robyn gently let go of one another and moved away from the fireplace.

Anna whispered "He doesn't know he's dead, what should we do Robyn? Do we tell him or leave him be?" Robyn replied "I think we leave him be Anna" who softly nodded her head in agreement and quietly said "I'm utterly drained! I heard his voice speaking inside my head and repeated out loud exactly what he said. I'll need to listen back to the film to know what came out of my mouth; I wasn't consciously aware of the words. Robyn, maybe we use this method again, but not here at the castle, I must rest to recover; I also need to eat right now to ground myself!"

I stopped filming; Robyn asked for me to turn my camera back on. In a piece direct to my camera she said "I feel the need to explain a few of my actions during what Anna and I just did. Bertie MacDonald asked me if I am a Sassenach, I have no idea how Anglo-English relations were in his time, so I instead opted to declare myself French as it rightly or wrongly seemed the least possibly offensive option. I called myself Robina to avoid any potential confusion regarding him identifying with my real name as female" after that I turned off my camera once more.

The walkie crackled into life "Nanette to Robyn, come in, over" she replied "Robyn here Nanette, over" she said "On camera one there were the multiple orbs all over on the chimney breast during your filming, over" Robyn answered "We shall be with you in a moment to all take a look at the footage from camera one. Anything else to report, over?" Nanette said "You all lost track of the time up there. It is the middle of the afternoon, chef sent us the cold buffet two hours ago, over" Robyn said "We are all done here, we shall pack away our gear and be with you in a minute Nanette, over and out!" she added to Anna "Please go now Anna, we shall pack everything away, you need to eat!" Anna didn't argue and went immediately.

After our late lunch in the control centre Nanette exclaimed "This is most bizarre; in the end our chimney sweep turned out to genuinely be called 'Bert' or more Bertie MacDonald! Anna, how are you feeling now?" Anna responded "For sure better for eating some food Nanette, but exhausted" she continued "This experiment works Robyn and we'll re-use it, but this is no way could I go through the experience again while we're here, it's unbelievably draining. I'm going up to my room to rest until dinner this evening, I'll have a shower to cleanse my aura, followed by a few gentle yoga stretches and then some sleep" wearing a concerned expression on her face, Robyn said "Anna, if you need anything at all text" Anna smiled warmly "Thanks Krásná, I will"

While Anna rested, and we took Romy for some fresh air in the late afternoon, as the rain had finally stopped; Nanette was on a personal mission, she went off in search of The Count. A little later in the day Nanette found me walking to retrieve a digital recorder we somehow accidently left in 'The Ballroom'; it's then she told me all about the initiative she had just undertaken on behalf of Anna and Robyn; she also shared The Count's reaction and the full conversation that took place.

She told me she asked a passing member of staff where to find The Count, and found him sitting in a high-backed chair relaxing reading a book in a small room overlooking the courtyard. Nanette formally said "Please may I talk with you Darling Count?" she told me The Count put down his book on a side table and he replied "Of course you may Darling Nanette, please take a pew! What's on your mind?" Nanette said she sat in an identical chair to The Count's, also angled to look across the courtyard. She told me she was determined to get straight to the point "I ask you to now please stop all of the flirting with Robyn and Anna all of the time Darling Count" she said The Count looked coolly over at her

"For you to take the trouble to find me and ask this of me you must have a jolly good reason; and as it's you sitting across from me making this request, am I to assume the ladies in question are blissfully unaware that you're here?" was his response. I know Nanette so well and was sure she wasn't in the slightest bit intimidated by The Count, she told me she quite openly admitted to him "No, they do not know I am here with you Darling Count" The Count apparently grinned and gestured with his hand for her to continue, she told me she said "Robyn and my cousin are the most deeply in love and devoted couple I ever know Darling Count, they are truly living for one another and it just seems not so nice of you flirting with Robyn in front of him. Naturally I observe Robyn is the exceptionally beautiful woman of the kind you rarely see, but she is also the delighted to be married exceptionally beautiful woman!" The Count inclined his head slightly in approval according to Nanette, and requested for her to continue "Anna; I am privy to the certain information I was never supposed to be hearing. Do not be ever asking me what this might be Darling Count; I keep this to myself forever. Please take my word on this one Darling Count; flirting with Anna is not such a good thing for you to do!" Nanette told me when the fixed cameras were running in 'The Ballroom' she heard all of the conversation between Anna and me, Nanette reiterated what she told The Count, she would never reveal a word of what she'd overheard to anyone.

She told me she then said "I'm trusting you Darling Count by requesting this of you and that you tell no-one I was here" Nanette said The Count arose to stand, indicating her to do likewise, bending over he took her right hand and kissed it, he said "Love for one's family and friends, along with the honour and loyalty you exhibit are all too rare Darling Nanette. Yes, in answer to your request. Forthwith I cease all my flirting; which please understand is largely borne out of my deepest respect for you! I tell you candidly Darling Nanette, you're quite a woman and I don't get to say that to many I meet" She left him to it then, and this is when she bumped into me, as she made her way back to her room.

Nanette looked me directly in the eyes "I am most sorry if I overstepped the mark Om; but I couldn't help myself! Watching The Count flirting with your Robyn was making the blood boil in my veins! I think that Anna is most vulnerable right now, she is discovering the new side to herself and maybe not quite understanding everything yet" I hugged Nanette "That was a beautiful thing you did for Anna and Robyn. You know I must tell Robyn about this Nanette? We have no secrets between us; but unless Anna ever specifically asks me why The Count now behaves differently, to her I shan't mention what you did on her behalf" Nanette looked relieved "Now I get ready for the dinner. Thank you Om for understanding why I did what I needed to!"

Arriving for dinner that evening confused Anna. Standing by the door as we entered the dining room The Count stood waiting and shook us each in turn by the hand as he welcomed us "'I don't believe I've enjoyed the pleasure of welcoming you all properly to my home; let's do this alphabetically shall we? Anna, it's an absolute pleasure to have you stay here at the castle as my guest. Darling Nanette, it's as much an absolute pleasure to have you stay here at the castle as my guest. Robyn likewise to you, it's an absolute pleasure to have you stay here at the castle as my guest. Mr Darke last but not least, it's an absolute pleasure to have you stay here at the castle as my guest!" Dinner proved a civilised affair; The Count behaved impeccably and proved the perfect host. Romy seemed to adore him and giggled every time he said something; his reaction was to stick his tongue out at her, this made her giggle even more! I confess I began to warm to him as well, when he didn't behave like the greatest gift to womankind, he was kind of fun to be around.

## 13

# THE COUNTESS MARY KNEW SHE WAS DEAD

It wasn't raining! Surprisingly for September in Scotland it proved a pleasant enough day for us to eschew jackets for the entire duration of our investigation outside of the castle.

Every single of the videos on our channel gets filmed on location. With our considerable collective experience; the challenges of filming in good light, poor light or even when under direct threat from paranormal nasties, we are able to deal with and kind of work around.

For all the time that we appear on-camera, there is at least quadruple this spent setting-up shots, occasionally doing re-takes and often lengthy discussions off-camera regarding where we need to go with the investigation. The previous day's shooting in 'The Ballroom' being a typical example. What would turn out after editing to be under a fifty minute video, took us practically five hours out on location to eventually complete everything to our satisfaction!

Shooting outside the castle proved our most challenging location yet! Uneven terrain, extremely dark conditions close by the wall contrasted with the bright sunlight as we moved a little further away. Nanette's job back in our hub was made much easier; we were only able to find level enough ground to set up one fixed camera!

It was squally; close to the castle wall it was nice and calm; walk a metre outside of this bubble and it was a challenge to stand up without getting blown over! We stayed close to the wall. Anna turned-up wearing this swing-style dress that couldn't have been less practical if it had tried, sans any make-up and her hair up in a high ponytail; she looked like some fan of jive who had time-travelled from her nineteen fifties rockabilly dance hall into the future to join us on a paranormal investigation.

"Greetings! This is Om Darke, alongside me as usual is the rather wonderful Robyn Humphries-Darke, and with us for the next few lockdowns we are thrilled to be joined by Anna Kostrová. This is the second in our series of three special paranormal lockdowns centred around this genuine medieval castle in Scotland. We were invited here by the owner for a week's long investigation of this incredible castle, his home! Here we venture outside of the castle itself for our lockdown; which finds us feeling tiny stood adjacent to these massive stone ramparts; Anna tell us why we need to investigate these walls" Anna talked directly into Robyn's camera "Many marauders attacked this castle across the centuries; not one of them managed to gain entry! This castle proved impregnable. Exactly where we are standing right now would have once stood warriors intent on taking the castle as their own; as death reigned down upon them from above. We are hoping to make contact with the restless spirits of these warriors!" Looking into Anna's camera, Robyn said "So the mission is clear Anna, and our lockdown begins"

Robyn's walkie buzzed into life "Nanette to Robyn, over" Robyn answered "Robyn here, what is it Nanette? Over" Nanette said "I watched on the camera one, I know the introduction is now in the can. The lovely photographer he sits here with me, he would like the permission to visit your location for 'just a moment' as he puts it, over" Robyn said "That is fine, as you said we have got through our introduction and are yet to be starting properly on the investigation, his timing is perfect. Thanks Nanette. Over and out"

"Good morning ladies and gent, I am most awfully sorry to disturb you! I know I promised I wouldn't need to, but I was just up there (He pointed to one of the turrets) the sun hitting my lenses made anything photographic impossible. I will go off to another turret later, before that I really need a banker-shot of you all down here if that is ok?" Anna answered "Yes, of course miláček, by the way, did I mention I am psychic? It comes as no surprise to me for you to be here, I already knew I would see you today! How do you want us to be posing?" he responded "Hmmm, the tall French lady in your hub is also a part of your team, be cool to get the four, oh actually five of you with the cute baby, all in the photo like when you arrived"

"Robyn to Nanette come in, over" After a moment's delay she answered "Nanette here. I hear his request on camera one; allow me the moment or two to be tidying myself up and getting Romy, and I join you forthwith! Over and out"

Anna said "You know my first name miláček, but in full I am Anna Kostrová; the blonde man stood over by the wall is Om Darke; the total babe with the body to die for kissing him is Robyn Humphries-Darke, they're married; the tall French lady is Nanette Fabienne and the cute baby is Romy Humphries-Darke" he replied "Thanks Anna, it's cool to put some names to faces. Romy is not Nanette's baby?" Anna confirmed that Robyn and I are Romy's parents. The lovely photographer said to Anna "You know as well as I do how this kind of light is tricky" she replied "We have only one fixed camera today for this reason, too light and too dark makes it, as you say, tricky".

Nanette arrived "I am not familiar with taking part the in lockdowns and I wish to present the authentic image of us; bearing all this in mind, how do you feel is best to proceed with the photo?"

"You know what Nanette, why don't we make this one an informal portrait? Natural please, not too much like you are posing and look at me if that feels comfortable"

He suggested "Anna, I want it to appear like you've just walked into the frame of the photo from the front" As she walked into shot he called out "Anna, look back over your shoulder at me" he grinned broadly at her to which Anna smiled back; exactly the image he wanted, with Anna in the foreground of the photo.

"Anna you are a delight to work with, and the camera loves you!" she responded "I'm a veteran of many photo shoots from being the fashion stylist for my mum, also called Anna Kostrová, she was a prima ballerina; I made this dress myself I'm wearing" Anna twirled to show him, now we got why she wore it. She added "You're a delight to work with too" with a shocked expression on his face he replied "You're seriously that beautiful, your mum was a prima ballerina and you make your own cool clothes?!" he pretended to faint onto the grass; to the considerable amusement of everyone.

After picking himself up, he said "I do my best Anna. I am all done and thanks again Anna; oh and actually all of you other ladies, Romy and gent as well!" he laughed at himself; we all joined in with his infectious laughter.

Robyn said "Tomorrow our investigation is down in the undercroft, beginning at ten" he responded "Cool; I'll see you all there. Bye Anna!" And with that he was gone. Anna declared "He is such an amusing man and really so very lovely!" Everyone laughed, Robyn of all people said what was clearly on all of our minds "Please you two just go now and get a room!" this is so not the kind of thing Robyn would normally dream of coming out with, which of course made it far funnier!

Castle cellars can be either the traditional dungeon or an undercroft, which is basically a storage area for wine, beer or other consumables. The castle we were investigating possessed both! Day one of this next lockdown would see us investigating the undercroft, day two the dungeon.

I said "Nanette, why don't you stay around and see first-hand one of our investigations? Romy will enjoy the fresh air and we'll warn you if you get close to being in shot" she replied "How thrilling! Thank you so very much! I will be doing my absolute best not to get in your way. Before you start, would anyone like a coffee? I need to retrieve my bag from the hub, in the process of which I grab for myself a coffee; I can equally easily return armed with the coffee for us all!" we all said yes to her offer, I talked to Romy while Nanette was away. She returned ten minutes later with the four coffees. She announced as she arrived "Chef tells me lunch is at the one o'clock; which is slightly over an hour away. I keep my eye on the time, allowing you to concentrate on your tasks in hand"

The next hour proved to be utterly fruitless. Robyn held her digital recorder repeatedly asking out loud "Is there anyone here who wishes to talk to us? Come forward and tell us your story, we mean you no harm" playback revealed absolutely nothing captured. Robyn decided to reach out psychically to contact any spirits who might be with us; to also draw a complete blank. Even Anna gave it a go, despite classic psychic work really not being her thing; also nothing came back to her.

## NANETTE SAVES THE DAY

Before starting our lunch Nanette asked "Might I make a suggestion?" Robyn replied "Oui Nanette! Anything at all to help would be most welcome!" Nanette offered "Why not switch your investigation up on to the top of the wall? Your questing for the invaders saw nothing; perhaps seeking to make the contact with defenders of the castle might prove more successful?" Robyn responded "That is a brilliant thought Nanette! We shall go back to the lower wall after lunch. Nanette please make this suggestion on-camera, we then debate your idea between ourselves and all agree to move location!"

We resumed filming outside the castle with Anna saying to camera "So far the spirits here elude us, we can't seem to make the breakthrough we need" at that precise moment Nanette appeared in shot, Anna continued "This is a rarity; Nanette Fabienne our technical director from our hub for this week joins us! Nanette, it is good to see you visiting us outside of your domain, what brings you down here?" Nanette replied into Anna's camera "I followed your lack of progress on the fixed camera Anna; might I possibly make the suggestion?" the three of us assented our approval "How about you move the location to up there?" Nanette pointed the perfectly manicured little finger on her right hand to the top of the wall "Your quest for invaders eludes your collective efforts, perhaps seeking the defenders of the castle proves to be the more fruitful?" Anna answered her "Nanette, that's actually a brilliant idea! What do you say Robyn and Darke, should we shift our focus onto to the top of the wall?" I said "Yes, sounds good to me. Robyn?" who affirmed "Nanette you have saved the day! Please do come along with us to join the lockdown up on the castle wall" This was unexpected and hadn't been discussed between us prior to Robyn's offer. Nanette was still on Anna's camera, she replied into it with a big smile "I would be most delighted to!"

A walkway ran all the way around the castle atop the wall. Observing the width of this walkway made it difficult to understand how this could have practically worked back in the day. The path was narrow, and with the guardrail put in place for modern health and safety concerns, it was just wide enough for two people to pass by one another. We put Romy in her pushchair out of shot where we could all see her, safely parked-up against a high turret wall. Pondering this main wall did make us all wonder how many stout defenders of the castle met their end through enemy fire, and how many of them accidently took one too many steps back to fall the twenty five metres backwards into the unforgiving courtyard below! Setting-up any fixed camera proved impossible without blocking all our own access for the investigation. Robyn, Anna and I each held a hand-held video camera; we took a digital recorder up there with us.

I introduced this new lockdown and Nanette. We nearly did an investigation together once before, but it never made it to film, finally I got to welcome Nanette to a paranormal investigation "Greetings! Anna, Robyn and I are now up on the top of the wall for this afternoon's lockdown; as suggested by Nanette Fabienne. I know some of you will ask, so to save you the trouble, Nanette and I are not actually twins, we're first cousins who just happen to look exactly like twins!" everyone laughed "Nanette; how does it feel to be on a lockdown for the first time?" Nanette replied "Om, I need to keep on be pinching myself to check this is for real. I avidly watch every single video of yours since the very first one you post; to find myself in one of your investigations is most surreal!" I smiled and suggested "Nanette, I think you should have the honour of being the first of us to see if you can capture an EVP"

In her cultured French accent Nanette said "Hello, my name is Nanette Fabienne, and these are my friends. Do you have anything you wish to say to us? We mean you no harm, we are simply desiring to know your story" after letting it run on for two minutes, Nanette then played it back "Countess" could be heard very faintly.

We cut filming. Anna said "There's a rumour one of The Count's ancestors jumped to her death from the castle wall. She'd be known as a 'Countess' oddly enough. It all got hushed-up. Few concrete facts are known, no pun intended. The question is do we continue?" I said "I'll text The Count asking him what he would like us to do" A few moments later The Count himself appeared in the courtyard below and strode up the steps up onto the wall to join us. "Great Grandmother was unhappy ladies and gent. I know little more than you about what happened, us gentry are excellent at going to ground to avoid scandals. Mr Darke, I would adore if you can find out more for me through your EVPs!" I replied "Count, this wasn't one of our EVPs, it was Nanette's!" Nanette said "Beginner's luck!" she continued "Darling Count are you sure you want us to be doing this? The video is posted to the most public channel where many millions subscribe" he smiled at her as he replied "Yes Darling Nanette I am quite sure, I am privy to none of the facts surrounding dear old Great Grandmother's death; you know I'm the only living descendant of hers? Might I make a suggestion?" Robyn answered "Fire away Count, do go for it, etc" The Count looked across at Nanette for a moment and then said "Darling Nanette, of all of us you are the most uniquely qualified to communicate with The Countess, she was French! She could open up more to you" I didn't bother mentioning the fact I am also French, anyway I agreed with him; Nanette would be more likely to get The Countess to respond.

For the record, the daughter of an Earl is known as Lady, his wife is generally known as The Countess. The Earl himself however is officially never known as The Count; although 'The Count' central to this story is an Earl and adopted this moniker. I admit this is terribly confusing; I didn't make the rules!

Nanette asked "What name was she known by Darling Count?" The Count replied "The Countess Mary".

I said "Count, stay for the duration if you like; I strongly ask you to remain off-camera and please stay absolutely silent while we're filming" he replied "Thanks awfully Mr Darke. I promise you won't hear a peep from out of me!" He went over to stand with Romy, who seemed delighted to see him and started giggling straight away;

he knelt down onto her level to talk with her and he didn't use 'baby talk' but spoke to her like she was an adult. He informed Romy how much he enjoyed their conversations and he always found himself fascinated listening to her opinions. Like I said earlier, by now I'd warmed to the guy and for sure Romy adored him; he didn't take himself too seriously, which was cool. He fell silent as we began filming.

In French Nanette said "This is Nanette Fabienne, are you The Countess Mary?" playing back caught the faint EVP in English "Party Dahling!" Nanette asked "Are you at a party?" Playing back it seemed we had captured nothing intelligible; Robyn later analysing on her laptop came up with "Left", which she took to mean The Countess Mary had left the party. Nanette said "Nanette Fabienne again Countess Mary, I am stood on the top of the castle wall, do you also ever come up here?" played back the word "Cheat!" was clearly heard. Nanette asked "Who cheated Countess Mary?" this time "Married" came through loud and clear. "May I ask you one French woman to another French woman, did your husband have the affair?" once more the word "Married" came through and after that no more EVPs; next it was down to us to possibly fill in some blanks.

Anna said "Robyn, let's do it again!" Robyn looked aghast "Are you absolutely sure you wish to do this Anna?" she smiled wanly and stepped closer to the wall, beckoning for Robyn to join her. Nanette said "I think I ought to be in Anna's shoes for this. I am of course not in the slightest trained as the psychic, yet The Countess Mary talked to me through EVPs. I believe she is more likely to open-up to me, she trusts me as another French woman" Robyn if possible looked more aghast "Nanette that plan is crazy! Anna is in danger enough and she is a highly experienced psychic! For you to attempt this is a ludicrous" Nanette suggested "How about we make a compromise? You and Anna do precisely as you did the last time, and I hold onto you both so we see if anything comes through me?" Anna and Robyn proclaimed in unison "No Nanette!" Anna added more softly "This is far too dangerous, we cannot risk you getting hurt de toute beauté"

They decided Robyn would ask the questions in French; and with that the two psychics hugging as before, with their heads closely together and relaxed. After a short while and somewhat less than the hour it took the day before, it began. I translate everything that was said into English for you.

Robyn – Are you here with us?

To everyone's shock Nanette answered – Yes Dahling.

Anna nearly broke off from Robyn, who held onto her even closer and tighter.

Robyn – Who do I have the pleasure of talking with?

Nanette – Countess Mary.

Robyn – Countess Mary. Are you on this wall with us?

Nanette – Obviously! I jumped off the thing!

Robyn – You know you jumped Countess Mary?

Nanette – You are the silly girl aren't you? Yes Dahling, I know I jumped off the wall and died!

Robyn – Why did you jump Countess Mary?

Nanette – Bored, so frightfully bored of everything!

Robyn – Why where you bored Countess Mary?

Nanette – The affair. The scandal. All so frightfully boring dear.

Robyn – What affair Countess Mary?

Nanette – Obviously I shall not tell you that you silly girl.

Robyn – Was it the Earl?

Nanette– Oh, you know. The scandal!

Robyn– The scandal was why you jumped?

Nanette– Can I trust you Lady Nanette?

Robyn – Of course Countess Mary!

Nanette – The only way Dahling, I had to jump, the scandal would ruin the family.

Robyn – It was you having an affair. Did the Earl discover this?

Nanette – Yes dear.

The séance met with an abrupt end as Nanette passed-out unconscious! I cut filming.

Robyn and Anna rushed to her aid. The Count moved past me to also help Nanette. I went over to check on Romy, she was sound asleep.

Nanette came around in only a few seconds, and smiled up at everyone "Sorry about the fuss and my apologies! Anna, I could not possibly allow you to be going through all that stress again so soon after only yesterday in 'The Ballroom'. I sensed I was most pivotal to this case. I knew if I stay close enough by you both The Countess Mary would talk through me. I feel exhausted; Anna you are quite right, this is most terribly draining!"

And with that the lockdown was over. I filmed a short ending conclusion piece assuring viewers Nanette was absolutely fine and with that we all left the wall.

The Spirits at Jim's Bar

# 14

# MURDER IN THE WINE CELLAR

Robyn and I discussed a plan, I needed to get the 'Bert' film edited and promptly. There was a press conference looming at the castle and it needed to be ready to show. No ifs, buts or maybes. Robyn suggested I sit out the final investigation; I could stay back in the hub working on the video and have Romy there with me. Robyn explained we already had the perfect replacement for me on lockdown, my 'twin'. This made so much sense to me I wondered why I hadn't already thought of it. I so love that woman!

At 9.30am we were all sat down in the hub, where I was in the process of briefing everyone "As this is the first day of our final two-part investigation, I want to do something different. I set camera one up there covering the desk of the hub, it films what goes on behind the scenes; which I edit into the video at the moments any action occurs" with an alarmed expression on her face Nanette stated "I am really not too sure about being filmed today Om! I didn't prepare for being in front of the camera, observe by my most ramshackle appearance!"

Despite her self-deprecation, Nanette's appearance is never 'most ramshackle'. She may not have worn her usual suit, and admittedly I am probably biased about my cousin; anyway I think she looked frankly amazing completely natural with her hair hanging down loose, dressed for comfort in her yoga sweats.

I explained "Nanette you are going to carry the walkie and communicate with me out on the investigation with Robyn and Anna. I am running the hub I need to get this 'Bert' film edited, I can also keep an eye on your progress and if needed walkie you to tell you anything significant. You will be more effective as part of the investigation than me Nanette. Lockdown begins in half an hour."

Robyn spoke first "It shall be strange you not being there alongside me babe; yet you would be far too distracted; I agree on this lockdown Nanette shall be considerably more effective than you. Next came a panicked Nanette "Argh! I wear the zero make-up and my hair it is à la Cathy haunting Heathcliff! I immediately dash to throw on a suit to create the illusion I made the modicum of the effort; I must put-up my hair and I need make-up! I promise I can do all of this is in under thirty minutes! I will be right back!" Nanette took off her shoes and literally sprinted from the hub up to her room. She did exactly as promised and returned in twenty eight minutes flat looking more typically her immaculate self.

Finally it was Anna's turn to voice her opinion "I trust in your judgement Darke".

Robyn told me that night about what happened as they strolled on their way to the undercroft; Anna briefly caught her eye, and then she said "We need to decide which of us will act as team leader in Darke's absence. I count myself out of the running, as a psychic it couldn't work" Robyn said that she pretended to ponder this "You know I have to agree with you Anna, I shall also count myself out of the running, us psychics cannot possibly lead the investigation" Nanette apparently stopped walking to stare in utter astonishment at them and she exclaimed "You are both aware I am beyond the mere novice when it comes to paranormal investigations and yet you consider me ideally qualified to fulfil the role as your team leader?!" Anna smiled at her and said "You're Darke's doppelganger and you share all of his presence, you're the only natural choice Nanette" Robyn said she added "Delighted this is all decided!" Nanette continued staring at them both, until with a resigned shrug of her shoulders she accepted the hand fate had dealt her "If you are so totally sure, I suppose I accept the majority decision" Anna and Robyn enveloped her in a group hug to celebrate achieving their goal. Robyn texted me that Anna and her discussed this matter of who would team lead in the ladies washroom before heading out to meet up with Nanette and walk down to the undercroft, neither of them wanted to take on the role of team leader in my absence, it didn't feel right to them. They reached the decision to nominate Nanette. They agreed Nanette would prove more than capable.

Having already been there to set up the fixed cameras I knew they would need to walk down two flights of steep stone steps to arrive in the subterranean area under the more recently built part of the castle; recently built in this case is a relative term. The original castle dates back to the twelfth century, but little of that survives. As with most ancient castles, new fortifications, together with new buildings got added on as required down through the centuries. The undercroft in question sits beneath an eighteenth century addition to the castle, it was and still is an extensive wine cellar, and these days also houses all the boilers and pipes for the heating system that warms the entire castle.

I'd been busy. Three fixed cameras greeted them when they reached their lockdown location. Camera two covered the main corridor; camera three panned across the massive wine cellar and in the boiler room is where camera four was located. I watched on camera two as Robyn looked around herself, she told me later she was reminded of the cellars back in Dover under Jim's Bar, although these were practically five times their size.

I watched Nanette switch on her walkie "Nanette to Om come in, over" I replied "I am here Nanette, I can see you on camera two. Over" Nanette waved to me and then asked "Om, where do you suggest we should be starting down here? Over" as Robyn had already texted telling all about Nanette's new role, I replied knowing my response would give her the confidence she needed "I have absolutely no idea Nanette. This is the team leader's decision and I completely trust you'll make the right choice. Over and out"

I watched on all my fixed cameras as Nanette walked solo through the entire undercroft complex and returned fifteen minutes later to talk with Anna and Robyn. She said "Ladies, the wine cellar seems the most superb place to commence our investigation. I film proceedings to free you both up to investigate without the need for you to also act as the camera women. Robyn I would like you to go for the EVP's and you Anna please reach out psychically into the essence of this structure and inform us if we are likely to be encountering anything negative. If your answer is in the affirmative, we investigate further" fascinated I watched on as Nanette become the team leader before my eyes.

I watched on fixed camera two. Nanette said "I need to be recording the introduction next, please film me now Anna" she was so professional, but Nanette was used to public speaking, so I guess this kind of thing she could do in her sleep "Hello everyone! I am Nanette Fabienne, standing in on this lockdown for my cousin Om Darke;

he is in the control hub for this investigation. Alongside me are the two paranormal investigators incredible; I am most fortunate to be surrounded by such capable women as lovely Anna Kostrová and Robyn Humphries-Darke! I am nominated by them as the team leader for our final investigation in Scotland. Once more we are exploring the spirit residents in this most incredible medieval castle for the owner. This investigation for the first time ever camera one is placed back in the control hub to offer the insight into what goes on behind the scenes. Mr Om Darke is running things back there; you will be seeing him many times throughout this investigation! This lockdown is to be in the two parts. This first part today sees us investigating one of two separate cellar areas beneath the castle, this storage area we are in here is known as the undercroft. In part two tomorrow we get to visit the dungeons! Anna tell us what we are hoping to discover during today's investigation" Anna spoke into Nanette's camera "This area where we stand Nanette is three hundred years old, I can't wait to see who wants to communicate with us. Nanette, where do we investigate first?" Nanette looked into camera two "Anna and Robyn, during my walk-through of this undercroft earlier I became especially drawn to investigate the wine cellar. The owner he has the most excellent taste, I notice most of the wines in there are French!" Anna and Robyn laughed, Nanette continued with "We begin there in the wine cellar.

Robyn please attempt to capture some of the EVPs and Anna might I ask you to be reaching out into the fabric of the walls to ascertain if there is anything demonic with us?" the introduction was in the can. I was so proud of Nanette and seriously impressed as well! For this case I'd created a live feed from Nanette's camera directly to her own laptop, which sat on the desk in front of me. I turned the link on so I would be able to follow them as they investigated.

At this moment the lovely photographer arrived "Good morning Mr Darke, where is Nanette?" I replied "Today she leads the investigation and I run the hub" he didn't seem too astounded at this news, he asked me "Is their investigation at a crucial point or can I pop down to capture a few snaps of them? Is Anna there with Nanette and Robyn?" I assured him she was. I picked up the walkie and said "Darke to Nanette, come in. Over" after a moment she replied "Hi Om, We are commencing with the investigating, am I correct in guessing the lovely photographer is with you? Over" I replied "Affirmative Nanette. Over" she said "Please do send him down. Thank you. Over and out"

Just for the record, as I am sure you will be wondering, yes Anna had dressed for the occasion again. She wore a pink floral maxi skirt and a cream embroidered top; both of which she probably made herself. Flat pumps on her feet emphasised her pettiness. Her face was once more devoid of any make-up and she had put her hair up in a bun. The Anna Kostrová I once knew would have been mortified to come across as either 'girly' or 'cute'; now she looked the embodiment of both.

I watched on camera two as Anna greeted him when he arrived "Do you have anywhere in particular you need to be for the next few hours?" she asked him "Not really Anna, why do you ask?" she replied "Rather than us posing around pretending to investigate, how about you join us on our lockdown for the opportunity to capture images of us going about our real investigation? You'll need to remain close by my side for the duration I'm afraid; you need to stay out of shot in the wine cellar. I will touch your arm to let you know you need to move away when I'm about to be filmed" He really couldn't have looked any more delighted at this prospect had he tried "Yes please; thank you Anna! You know, needing to remain close by your side for several hours will be tough for me, however I shall bravely attempt to cope with the hardship" Anna laughed delightedly at his dry humour. Nanette and Robyn got no say in this one; and they both told me after the lockdown they wouldn't have dreamt of getting in the way of Anna and her very public courtship with the lovely photographer.

The lovely photographer asked Anna "May I catch a quick photo of you all in this corridor where Nanette did your intro, before you get too deeply into investigating wine and spirits?" Anna laughed at his joke and she answered "Yes, of course!"

I watched on camera two as everyone continued with business as usual. Nanette took a camera to film some scene-setting shots of the entrance to the wine cellar from outside in the corridor. Robyn stood centrally looking far into the middle distance deeply within the same waking meditation I too use when preparing to face the unknown on case. Anna talked with the lovely photographer as he set up his shot and she found herself unwittingly placed even more prominently this time right there in the foreground.

The arrived in the wine cellar and rather usefully for me, following their progress, Nanette's camera now went live to her laptop. I watched as she filmed Robyn going for EVPs "Is there anyone here with me? I only wish to talk, I mean you no harm, please communicate with me" She repeated this several times, with the usual minutes' pause to allow for any responses. Playing back the recording there was faintly heard a refined male voice quite clearly saying "Spoiled vintage". They looked at one another. Robyn went once more through her routine of asking for EVP responses from the spirits, playing back this time they heard a female voice with a strong Scottish accent say "Aye".

Robyn continued asking for communication, but they got no more voices coming through for the moment. I watched on Nanette's camera as Robyn decided to see if she could pick-up on anything psychically. She said "I sense a young woman, more of a girl; she is dressed like a servant. She looks around her" after a few moments she continued "She died on that spot" Robyn pointed to the floor around a metre in front of where they stood. She asked "And yet how can she possibly have died so young?" she then announced "She is gone now. I cannot sense anything else; I shall maybe try again a little later. Anna did you get anything?"

She replied to Nanette's camera "Nanette asked me to see if I could sense any evil here; like negative entities or even anything demonic. While you were EVP'ing I went over to touch the walls and feel outwards. Nothing truly evil came through, but something decidedly unpleasant happened down in this wine cellar ladies. I believe you and I now possess a good idea of what this might have been Robyn. Yes?"

Robyn said "Yes Anna, I know exactly what you are thinking about. We need some real evidence to be sure Anna and at the moment this eludes us"

Nanette said into her own camera "We are investigating the wine cellar, some fascinating details about the spirit entities occupying this place already emerge, yet for now at least it seems the progress it has stalled. We now move locations to the other end of the cellar, furthest away from the door and see if we are able to get back on the trail once more!"

They were off-camera, so I had no idea what was going on. I decided to keep watching camera three to see if anything interesting showed up in the wine cellar, I wasn't to be disappointed. Robyn told me that night her and Nanette went over into a corner to discuss the best way to proceed; Nanette asked for her opinion on how Anna and Robyn herself would re-establish contact with the spirits; so she could make the appropriate decisions as team leader to move the case forward.

Anna told us later what had happened whilst Robyn and Nanette had their planning meeting, when she and the lovely photographer found themselves all alone. They smiled at one another. She said that despite being fully aware of how complicated this might get all too soon, he told her that evening he had no choice and must do it; he couldn't risk Anna walking away in a few days to never see her again! In a low voice he asked her "Anna, do you like Italian food?" equally quietly she answered "To the absolute excess!" he finally asked what he had wanted to since the first moment he clapped eyes on her wearing her kilt when she arrived, he whispered "Anna, there is this amazing restaurant in town, it's only ten minutes' walk from the castle gates, would you like to forgo chef's effort here tonight and come with me to sample the undisputed finest pasta this side of the Scottish Border?" Anna said she looked him in the eyes, to quickly break into a big smile as she whispered in his ear "Yes! I would really love to do that with you! Please can we keep this date to ourselves for now?" the lovely photographer grinned in delight and winked at her in his agreement.

Nanette's walkie sprang into life, I said "Darke to Nanette, over" who responded "Nanette here, over" I said "I saw a shadow figure on camera three, half way down aisle two of the wine racks, you're all off camera three right now so I am not too sure of your exact location, over" Nanette answered "Robyn and I were off in the far corner making a plan, I am thinking we need to be investigating this shadow figure most urgently, thanks for that Om! Over and out"

They were back on my camera three; I could see what was happening once more. And then Nanette's camera came back on. Nanette said "Ladies, I am sure you heard Om Darke. Robyn do you want to EVP this or go the whole psychic instead?" Robyn replied "Psychic will be more effective this time Nanette" who nodded and added "Anna please investigate more about those negative feelings you are getting to see any further details" Anna said "Nanette, we'll get to the bottom of this case! I'll be doing as you suggested and wandering around this cellar seeing if I'm able to unravel more about these negative vibes I strongly feel" The lovely photographer mouthed to Nanette as he pointed to them in turn "U on R, me on A?" her thumbs-up and smile confirmed her agreement to his plan. Picking up their spare camera he was ready. I watched all their footage later.

Nanette filmed Robyn as she went straight along to the location where I'd witnessed the shadow figure on camera three. She closed her eyes "I sense the same girl once again. She is waiting for a man. Oh my gosh! I understand everything now!" Robyn opened her eyes and said to Nanette "Anna shall solve the other half of this mystery and only then we can explain all!"

Anna walked slowly around the whole of the cellar until she stopped by one of the oldest wine racks in the cellar, looking into the lovely photographer's camera she said "He waited here" she continued with walking, adding "They argued here" this was only a few metres away from where Robyn said the girl died.

A few minutes later they were all back together, as Nanette filmed "Do you want to tell this or should I" Robyn asked Anna "Go for it!" Anna responded to her. Robyn began "Shortly after this cellar was constructed an awful event played out. A servant girl was engaged in an affair with one of the officers stationed at this castle. They would meet down in this cellar to express their passion. This lasted until the unfortunate day the girl announced herself to be pregnant. This officer would lose face with his men for getting a mere servant girl with child. In such a horribly calculating way he enticed the girl back down into the cellar one final time, which is when he murdered her right there!" Robyn once more pointed to the same spot as earlier.

The lovely photographer also continued with his filming, he turned his camera onto Nanette as her walkie crackled into life "Darke here, over" she asked "You were listening to all of that Om? Over" I replied "I watched the whole thing and quickly looked it all up on my laptop. A servant girl got reported missing by the housekeeper, she was never found and was presumed to have run away from the castle with her lover. Over" Robyn took the walkie and asked "Babe, is there a list of the officers stationed here at that time? I said "Negative Robyn, I searched. Nothing is listed. Over" Robyn said "Thanks babe, over and out"

Nanette announced "I observe it rapidly approaches 1pm, our lunch break is upon us. Rendezvous in the boiler room at 2pm. Thank you team!" she applauded Anna and Robyn.

Robyn and I had never been apart on any investigation. We fully appreciated Nanette was doing an exceptional job as team leader, but it felt too weird not being out there beside one another. Upon Robyn's arrival in the hub I picked-up Romy and we three hugged forever. I began to doubt my own judgement in taking on this case. I wasn't enjoying the feeling of watching Robyn on a screen rather than being with her and it felt horrible. I resolved to never again put myself into the professional position where it meant being apart from Robyn. I knew I had commitments I still needed to get through on this lockdown "We will soon be free of this!" I kept central within my thoughts, keeping me motivated. Frankly the 120k fee we were getting wasn't worth the compromises; anyway we made considerably more than that from our vids!

## TURNING THE HEAT UP

They reconvened at 2pm in the boiler room. Camera four I had set-up covering the wide open area that meets you when entering the room. The rest I would have to view from the live feed from off of Nanette's camera.

Nanette panned her camera around the room for some establishing shots and then turned it onto Anna and Robyn. I saw a new side to her as I listened; Nanette said "Putting aside the noise, it has to be at the minimum of thirty five degrees in this room with these boilers, pipes and heating thingies! Would you mind strolling around this entire room together? I follow alongside filming you;

please feel free to comment upon anything you sense ladies. After which I do the introduction, once we have already established some of the potential targets. With all our fingers crossed, some of the lucky heather and the dose of wild optimism this time there won't be anything at all in to investigate and we can move away to some other place quieter and cooler!" they all laughed and so did I back in the hub; Anna added "Try to think cold thoughts; we're all sat on an iceberg with a friendly polar bear; drinking a chilled gin and tonic!" they all laughed again; setting off to begin their walk through.

Nanette filmed them trying to concentrate on their tasks under duress, when suddenly the walkie crackled into life. I had just seen something! "Darke to Nanette, over" she replied "Nanette here, over" I said "I saw a shadow figure clearly on camera two literally a moment ago out in the main corridor. Over" Nanette laughed as she responded to this news "Thanks for that Om. Oh dear, we now must immediately abandon investigating in this deafening and steamy boiler room ladies to go directly to where Om saw this shadow. What an awful shame! Over" I replied "I got how a hostile an environment it is when I placed camera four in there. I can't hear anything at all on it over the sound of the boilers!" Over" Nanette in relief finished with "Merci for rescuing us! Over and out"

## MAKE IT GO AWAY

Nanette spoke into camera two "Hello once again, I am Nanette Fabienne still standing in for Om Darke, with me of course are the most gorgeous Anna Kostrová and Robyn Humphries-Darke. Back in our hub Om Darke just saw a shadow figure in this corridor we stand in. As promised earlier, we investigated the boiler room off-camera, before doing the filmed lockdown in there and nothing paranormal to report is evident. This of course does happen, however we do still need to investigate everywhere, even if we end up eliminating some of them. We focus now on the main corridor of the undercroft; as I mentioned Om Darke saw a shadow figure here on camera two. Robyn and I are both in agreement that this is the one for our expert demonologist Anna!" Nanette panned across to her" Anna, are you getting anything paranormal?" Anna spoke into the camera "Yes Nanette! I'm sense far down under where we're stood there is underground water, like a spring or a stream. Water acts as a medium for negative energies to lurk or travel in. When we were in here earlier I felt nothing negative; but now something demonic occupies this corridor and it's fully aware of us being here. Darke, I know you can see and hear us in the hub, walkie me now please miláček and we can talk this through!"

"Darke to the lockdown team, over" Anna said "It looks like I need to exorcise a demonic creature Darke, but the owner asked we only find out more about his ghosts. What do we do? Over" I replied "You need to exorcise it Anna! We have a duty to protect everyone else. Over" Nanette said "Thank you for this cousin, we did not know quite what to be doing next because of the agreement to not interfere with the spirits, over" I said "This is the exception to the rule ladies; and I take full responsibility. Anna, please go kick the ass of the demon! Over" Anna came back on the walkie "This might well be my last time ever doing this kind of thing Darke. Thanks miláček. Over and out"

I addressed Romy who was sat alongside me watching the screen "Romy, let's go outside for some fresh air!" I put her in her pushchair and we made our happy way out into the pleasant afternoon sun. We had a lovely stroll around the courtyard. The lockdown of course would continue to its conclusion regardless of me sat there watching it unfold. Our daughter getting a good night's sleep was far more important; some nice fresh air could only help her. In my absence Anna said into camera two directly to me "Wish me luck Darke!" and with that said, she began to do her thing.

As I mentioned before, we never show the exact process any of us goes through to cleanse a space of ghosts or evil entities. Anna did her thing; Robyn joined in with her as she had already experienced Anna in action and knew how she worked.

Nanette's and camera two filmed on in my absence; Romy and I really enjoyed our walk.

Day one of our two part lockdown was over.


## ANNA AND NANETTE SHARE SECRETS

Nanette came along to our room to tell Robyn and me all about a conversation she and Anna had just had; she also wanted to reveal some secrets of her own. Anna asked Nanette to share all with us, she didn't want to be the one to do this, and was pleased for this role to fall to Nanette.

She told us straight after the lockdown Anna quietly said to her "Nanette, I need to talk with you. Can we go up to the privacy of your room please?" she replied "Yes, of course Anna. I need to be talking with you as well!"

They were now up in Nannette's room, she asked "Do you want to go firstly Anna?" she apparently looked shyly at Nanette "The lovely photographer invited me out for dinner tonight at an Italian place in the town, I said yes Nanette. I know this is insane, we live at different ends of the country, but you know I really like him Nanette. And I mean a lot!" Nanette said Anna sat there staring at her waiting for some reaction. She told us she said "I believe it is my turn now Anna" what she said next certainly surprised us, we had no idea! She told Anna "I have been meeting with The Count, Peter he asks me to call him, early every day before the lockdowns and every evening after dinner. This is only to be talking, Peter is the total gentleman and we are getting along most well. He texted me as we ate our lunch today offering to cook the meal for us in his private quarters. I agreed this would be most pleasant, this is tonight and of course, this takes us onto being in a relationship!" At this revelation we hugged Nanette; and truthfully said we were delighted for her. Robyn and I looked at one another for a moment and then smiled, Robyn said "This feels right Nanette" she cried a little and agreed she felt right about it too.

Back in Nanette's room, Anna asked "Nanette, are you kind of looking for my blessing to date Peter?!" Nanette replied "Om and Robyn have each other; I confess I feel the closest to you Anna as the two single women. Oui, I really would be liking your blessing Anna!" who replied "Yes beautiful, you've sure got it!" Nanette responded "That means a lot to me. Anna why did you tell me about your date? Do you want the blessing from me?" Anna said "Oui Nanette, s'il vous plaît" she told us she responded "Anna, your two's sexual chemistry has been driving the rest of us mostly up the wall! Please go to have lots of the sex with him to give us all the peace!" They laughed and hugged. Anna asked Nanette to talk to us and explain everything; then she went off to get ready for her date. We suggested Nanette might like to go and do the same, she agreed with this and off she went as well.

We sat with Romy and apart from each other, we were all alone in the dining room. I said to Robyn "Say Nanette and The Count is not some holiday romance and so they become an item, and the same with Anna and the lovely photographer; where does that all leave us and paranormal investigation? They cannot possibly commute down to Kent every time we have a case!" Robyn smiled as she asked the game-changer "Wouldn't you rather we got back to our simpler times babe? When only we two were the team and we loved every single moment we spent together on a lockdown" I smiled at my wife and answered "Yes babe. Yes I would".

# The Spirits at Jim's Bar

## 15

# DOWN IN THE DUNGEON

We sat in the hub, the lockdown team were getting themselves ready to head out and we were enjoying a coffee beforehand.

I said "I don't need to tell you the dungeons is the big one ladies!" Nanette replied "I never imagined when we arrived here at the castle I find myself appointed team-leader. It is like I am dreaming and soon I awaken!" I smiled warmly at my incredible cousin "You're a revelation Nanette, you rose to the situation perfectly, but then I know you and never expected less. Cousine adorée, you do everything excellently; apart perhaps from choosing locations to investigate!" Nanette and Robyn laughed; Romy joined in with them".

Looking across from behind my desk at them all I said "I am excited at see what you discover today ladies!" Anna told us "The lovely photographer is going to be meeting us down there from the start, as with yesterday he shall follow our investigation to take his photos, and he offered to help us out by filming this morning" I added "He's been emailing his photos each night, which I post to our social media, when you have a moment check out the many comments; seems our followers cannot wait to see our new Scottish videos. Please be safe and enjoy the lockdown!" Robyn and I hugged and kissed; and with a heavy heart I watched her walk off for the lockdown with Anna and Nanette.

## WALKABOUT AND MAKING CHOICES

Robyn told me over breakfast she had the feeling this day would prove our most fruitful yet at the castle.

I'd already placed all my fixed cameras in-situ. Camera two sat in the main largest room of the dungeon. Camera three covered this particularly gruesome cell in the dungeons. Camera four was situated in the oubliette (bottle dungeon). The oubliette originally had the typical entrance at the top from which prisoners would once have been dropped many feet down into the cell; in the late twentieth century a passage got cut through to afford easier access through a door into the room.

The lovely photographer volunteered to film for us, this would free all the team to investigate unencumbered with any equipment. His camera, which was Nanette's, still linked to her laptop, which sat in front of me on my desk. I could follow everything that happened all morning, whilst also keeping an eye on my fixed cameras, working on the 'Bert' video and spending some quality time with Romy who sat alongside me in her high-chair. Busy? Kind of!

I noticed on camera two the lovely photographer arriving early. He stood waiting for the team to arrive. They soon did. Anna immediately embraced him and they began to kiss. After ten minutes Nanette smiled at Robyn and said "Most sorry to interrupt you when you are busy, we are both actually here as well!" Anna and the lovely photographer laughed, he said "Apologies and a jolly good morning to you ladies!" Robyn was curious about something, she asked "You are clearly not Scottish, how did you end up living here?" he replied "The Count and I are old friends, when he started his wedding business here at the castle he asked me to film and photograph these events for him. I lived in Manchester and at first I stayed up here at the castle in one of the rooms you're using. Long story short, l fell in love with the town and moved up here permanently two years ago. My office is in the admin area of the castle" Nanette asked him "How did you get into the photography?" surprisingly he replied "I think of myself as essentially an artist Nanette, although photography pays my bills. I studied at University in Manchester, I enjoy it most of all when I can get creative through painting" Anna put her arm around him "Perhaps you shall one day be able to paint for your living?" he gently stroked her hair as he answered "That's an interesting idea Anna. I paint for only pleasure now but I would love to make it my profession"

I continued watching on camera two as Nanette shared her ideas for their investigation "My plan is we do the walk through of the entire dungeon complex together as a group this morning, the lovely photographer he films us. Needless to be said we are required to be remaining conscious of staying in close proximity to one another then he gets us easily all in-frame. We comment or react to anything ghostly or even ghastly encountered!" everyone laughed, I had no idea Nanette possessed such a silly sense of humour and I loved this new side to her I was discovering. She continued "After lunch we each venture out armed with a camera for a solo vigil in the most creepy rooms, we keep our walkies handy in case we are quickly in need of the help" Robyn suggested "Nanette feel free to do your wonderful introduction whenever you are ready"

Nanette indeed did her wonderful introduction as she was ready "Hello everyone and welcome. I am Nanette Fabienne, alongside me of course are the gorgeous Anna Kostrová and Robyn Humphries-Darke; I am standing in as team leader for Mr Om Darke, he is back in our control hub as our extra pair of eyes. This is to be the final day of our investigation in Scotland at this incredible medieval castle. We saved the creepiest to last; today our lockdown sees us deep down in the dungeons under this castle! Anna please inform us what are you expecting to discover today" she looked into the lovely photographer's camera "Nanette, I don't need to tell you that this location doesn't possess a very pleasant history. What do I expect us to discover? To be honest, some pretty grim stuff! Nanette, what's the plan for today?" Nanette next seriously looked like she was delivering a case summary to a judge as she talked directly into the lovely photographer's camera "I am wanting us to be doing all the justice today to this amazing opportunity. Later we shall each of us venture off for a solo vigil armed only with a video camera each. Before that, this morning we have the group walk through the entire complex; this helps us each decide where we go later for our solo lockdowns. For this first part of our lockdown we are fortunate enough to have procured the services of the lovely photographer who is filming me at this moment, he continues to film us all of the morning, he shall leave us too it once we go solo. I am not blessed to be a trained psychic like you Robyn and Anna, and yet even I feel the oppressive energy permeating throughout this entire area" Nanette smiled warmly as she turned to face her team "Ladies, let us begin our investigation!"

All of the accoutrements of the dungeon's past use were long gone; more than likely removed over at least a century before by an ancestor of The Count who perhaps wanted to leave behind some of his ancestor's less savoury practices. The oppressive energy of despair remained throughout the dungeons.

One enters the whole dungeon complex down a long dark corridor to emerge into a now well-lit large room, which once upon a long time ago would have been the location of all said accoutrements for gaining confessions of guilt from unfortunate prisoners. Off this main room, another corridor leads to the cells; and in an annexe off this corridor and down steep steps can be found the modern door cut into the oubliette.

The lovely photographer filmed the three women from the large room as they emerged out into it from the entrance corridor. Nanette was saying "I am aware you are both the psychics; in particular Robyn, if you feel yourself getting overwhelmed by the negativity in here I want you to leave immediately. Clearly and obviously this applies to you as well Anna, and yet as you are attuned more to sense any dark forces, you are perhaps more able to remain detached than Robyn; would that be fair to say?" Anna answered "Yes, it would for sure Nanette. Already a wave of negativity washes over me. I've got my protection, as we all have, even the lovely photographer, hopefully we shouldn't find ourselves too badly affected. I guess we'll see!" Robyn added "I appreciate all of your concerns Nanette; I promise if it gets a too oppressive for me I shall leave"

Unexpected loud banging noises came from somewhere within the room, all three women screamed in surprise "Where did those noises originate from?" Nanette asked; Anna replied "I feel the past all around us! Please follow me, the sound came from over there!" they walked a few metres to stand in front of a wall. Fresher cement stood out as clearly visible within the stonework above head height, Anna said "The noises came from here, I see men shackled to this wall, do you also get anything Robyn?" who answered "This is too horrible; yes Anna I feel the pain, but I cannot see the men as you do" Nanette asked "Is there anything we are able to be doing right now to help these poor souls from the past?" Anna replied "Nanette, this is one of those past emotional events projected into the future through stone memory scenarios. We can't change what happened, it's done and this isn't a case of the spirits of these men trapped here Nanette, these events happened long ago and we can't change that"

Robyn had gone incredibly pale "Are you okay Robyn?" asked the lovely photographer; he really hadn't intended interacting with the team but was concerned she looked like she was about to faint. Anna put her arm around her for support "I feel weird, may we all move away from this wall?" They walked into the centre of the large room, Robyn said "I am okay to stay Nanette; over by that wall there was something affecting me, I feel okay now we are away from there" I guess you can imagine how I felt at that precise moment sitting helplessly in the hub! I had also witnessed something…

Their walkie crackled into life "Darke to Robyn, Over" they all jumped in surprise, Nanette handed her the walkie "Robyn here babe. Over" I said "Shadow figure clearly visible a moment ago on camera two, a metre or so behind where the lovely photographer is right now. When you were over by the wall an orb went into you babe, and came back out when you moved away. Over" they looked at one another. Robyn responded "Thank you babe, good to know it went!" I finished "All of you please be careful; including you the lovely photographer! Over and out"

Anna was about to be anything but careful. For all her girly girl new image and sweet fresh-faced appearance, some things never change! That woman simply cannot help herself…

Nanette turned on her digital recorder. "Hello my name is Nanette Fabienne; these are my friends Anna and Robyn. Does anyone here wish to communicate with us? We mean you no harm, simply to talk and know of your story" she repeated this several times, obviously leaving a suitable gap in-between to allow for any responses; she played it back. She had captured a few EVP's "No" "Go Away!" and "Leave!" were all heard loud and clear. They looked at one another. With a wink, Anna took the digital recorder from her and said "No! We are not going away or leaving! You'll need to do better than that to scare us away!" Another loud bang reverberated around the room. With the digital recorder still switched on for EVP responses, Anna shouted "Do your worst \_\_\_\_\_! We don't scare easily!"

Anna said delightedly "Let's play this one back to see if I got anything else when I provoked the evil spirit". They heard "Scare!" and "Run. Anna immediately shouted "We are NOT scared or running! We stay as long as we want!"

Nothing further got captured on EVP in response to Anna's latest provocation. She addressed Robyn and Nanette "This is where I need to do my solo vigil later ladies; I can't resist wanting to know more about an entity who wants to scare me away!"

The lovely photographer followed as they eventually left the larger room and began walking down the corridor to the cells. Behind them they all clearly heard a deep growl emanating from the room behind them. Anna shouted back into the empty space "I'll be back to see you later all on my own!"

There were three main cells, and a narrow passage leading down to the oubliette. The pungent aroma of damp pervaded the air as they entered the first cell. I had been there before them to place my camera three.

Picking up the walkie Nanette said "Nanette to Om, Over" I replied "Yes Nanette? Over" she asked me "I wondered why you choose this cell out of all of them to place the camera three. Over" I replied "As I went down earlier this morning setting-up I met a maintenance man adjusting the outer door to make it easier for you to open. We got talking and he came along with me while I placed my cameras. It was this man who suggested the cell you are now in as he himself had a scary experience in there! Over" Nanette replied "Wow! Thank you Om. Over and out"

She addressed her team "I have chosen the location for my solo vigil ladies, for some reason this room it is creeping me out so much, I return here later by myself to ascertain why!"

Robyn said "You know on or off-camera we have yet to visit the oubliette? I personally feel drawn to investigate the location. Please may we not explore it together Nanette? I would like to go there solo for my vigil and be the first of us three to see it; with no preconceived ideas regarding what I shall uncover" When I set my camera four up in there I kind of knew Robyn would later choose this place for her solo vigil.

Nanette addressed the lovely photographer's camera "Ladies we each have the locations for our solo vigils. I feel sure they chose us rather than us choosing them, we see later what the rest of this lockdown brings. Thank you everyone!"

And with that said the morning's investigation was through, they all headed back to the hub and a break for lunch. The lovely photographer left them at this point; obviously only after several minutes spent locked in a passionate embrace and kissing Anna.

I welcomed them back and congratulated Nanette for the exceptional work as team leader.

I addressed them all "We all know soon is Press and Media Day; I need to premier our first video from the castle. I am mostly finished with editing the 'Bert' case video; but I need to record some voice-overs which are going to have to be completed in the quietness of our bedroom; we know with the window closed no sound travels in or out of any of them, the soundproofing is quite extraordinary! Romy is shortly due her afternoon nap, which makes things easier.

I continued "I cannot monitor the hub for this afternoon. I apologise ladies. I must get the 'Bert' video completed and ready. I won't have time tomorrow" Robyn hugged me, followed by Anna and then Nanette; who assured me "We shall be fine, we have our walkies and one another's backs down there. Best of luck cousin!"

TRANSCRIPT FROM SOLO VIGILS - 2.15PM THROUGH TO 3.10PM, THE COUNT'S CASTLE IN WEST SCOTLAND

Anna – I'm here for my solo vigil in what, back in the mist of time, was the room used to extract confessions from poor prisoners, and by whatever means necessary. This now empty space would once have echoed to the screams of pain being inflicted. In our earlier group walk through I personally interacted with a spirit who wanted us all to leave. I said we stay! As we did eventually go off to explore another area, we all clearly heard a growl, which got caught on camera. I promised this entity I would be back later all on my own. Hi Honey, I'm home!

Robyn – I have never been in this oubliette before. The energy is truly awful in here, not surprisingly I guess. For those of you unfamiliar with oubliettes, this room originally would only have had that trap door I am now showing you up there in the roof. Prisoners would be dropped into this dungeon from that trap door. If they survived the fall, for sure bones would be broken from the impact; food was thrown down to them periodically. They would be in pitch darkness most the time. As I explain this, I can sense multiple spirits all around me.

Nanette – I do not mind admitting to you I am mostly petrified! This cell I am in smells damp, lichen grows on the walls and the atmosphere in here it feels particularly horrendous.

Anna – Ohh, a loud bang from in that corner, I'll walk over to investigate. It's icy cold, brrr. Tell me your name! I know you're not a demon so you can growl at me as much as you like and you won't convince me you're demonic; all your growling won't scare me out of here! Speak to me like you did to us on our device earlier, use words instead of all that stupid growling.

Robyn - Please, one at a time! I cannot possibly listen to you all at once, it is overwhelming for me. I am getting the name Robert. Communicate with me Robert; make a noise if you are aware of me. Oh, okay. You heard that tap then as well as I did! Robert, was that you? Please tap again if it was. Tap once more. Thank you Robert. How many of you are there in here with you Robert? Please tap how many if you can. Silence. Oh, of course, Robert might not be able to count. Robert tap again if there is more than you in here. A tap! Thank you Robert!

Nanette – Against all logic I feel I ought to turn-off the light in this cell to switch over to the night vision on my camera. Viewers I am the most utterly petrified; I hear a noise sounding remarkably like the breathing from floor level. Eek! I quickly turn the light back on! Please speak to me spirit person, I mean you no harm and I only hope you feel the same way about me!

Anna – Ahh, I know who you are! You can't keep stuff from a psychic! You were the dungeon master, weren't you? Stop pretending you're a demon; I know far more about demons than you do, you _____ idiot. Growl! Growl! See, I can do that as well. Let's talk in growl language shall we? I'll say growl and then it's your turn. Growl, did you say? Oh you beat me to it. Oh, I'm sorry, am I supposed to be scared by that? Growl to you as well!

Robyn – Robert, are you still here with me? I don't like the feeling in here at all now. I have an instant headache and my feet hurt. Thank you Robert for communicating with me. I am leaving!

Nanette – Did I imagine or did a voice speak to say hello to me? Mon dieu! Okay, here goes, hello I am called Nanette, I am French, this is why I talk with the accent; can you tell me your name please? The name Morag popped into my head. I go with this. Is that you Morag? A tapping noise came from the floor. Are you on the floor Morag? Mon dieu it is cold!

Anna – Please stop growling at me, it doesn't scare me in the slightest. Make all the banging and crashing noises you like; I know when a spirit such as you could harm me and you sure can't! I'm getting bored now with your growling. If you won't talk to me then I'm going.

Robyn – I'll stay in the corridor, I hear Nanette and Anna are still in their lockdowns. I feel safer here. The oubliette proved too active, the challenge was discerning one voice amongst all the noise. Robert communicated with me and that alone made this lockdown worthwhile for me!

Nanette – Thank you Morag! If that really was you, please would you mind the tapping again? Yes! Thank you!

Anna – You had your chance moron. You're too stupid and _____ boring. I'm off to find my friends. Bye!

Nanette – I openly walkie Robyn and Anna "Ladies, I have the communication going on, if you are able, please join me! Over"

Nanette - I heard the name Morag in my head and went with it, she is easily tapping in response to my questions

Robyn - Reaching out into the ethers I get the sense of practically a young girl. She lays down on the floor unable to stand up. Oh no ladies, she is accused of witchcraft!

Anna - I sense this too Robyn. Do we all agree that Morag deserves to move on?

Robyn – We need to make the call on this, we cannot text Om, it would be unfair. Although, of course, knowing him he would probably come down here to join us! I say we help Morag to move on.

Anna – As I said, she deserves to move on. Nanette?

Nanette – Oui, most definitely. We have no choice.

Robyn did a Shamanic ritual cleansing ritual or as she would describe it, her Shawomanic cleansing ritual, allowing Morag to move on from that place to find peace.

Nanette addressed Anna's camera "This investigation in the dungeon concludes all our investigations at this spectacular castle in the most beautiful Scotland. If you loved this case please like the video and as always, we invite you to also subscribe to our channel to get all the latest notifications. Thank you for watching our Scottish cases, we all hope you enjoyed them."

GUIDED TOUR

The next day we spent with The Count, as we took him for a guided ghost tour of his own castle explaining what we'd discovered and where. We talked at length with him about all we encountered and answered his considerable number of questions.

When we got to the dungeon Anna, Nanette and Robyn explained about Morag, they also admitted between them they made the call to help her move on "Jolly good ladies, I am delighted you did this for Morag, had you been able to consult with me there and then, I would have suggested precisely the same course of action!" Nanette kissed him, which I confess did seem kind of strange to the rest of us; I never saw The Count looking quite that happy and relaxed. Once the tour was over he hugged each of us in turn, and gifted Romy a present of beautiful wooden hand-carved building blocks; and then hand in hand with Nanette off he walked towards the private area of the castle. I wouldn't miss that castle at all when we left, but The Count was an okay guy. It felt good for me to know Nanette was with Peter; as only she got to call him. It wasn't his responsibility I found myself apart from Robyn for the latter part of the investigation, for sure that one was all on me!

PRESS AND MEDIA DAY

The penultimate day of our week-long stay saw Press and Media Day finally upon us. The Count stayed away for this, it was never the intention he become a part of it; the whole idea of this event was for the press to meet us and allow them the opportunity to ask us questions.

Nanette is there anything we may do to support you?" this question was posed by Robyn. In only two hours the press and media would be descending upon the castle to see the thankfully completed 'Bert' video, after which they would be able to ask the team questions; there would later also be interviews for television, radio and newspapers.

We all knew before signing onto the investigation at the castle there would be a Press and Media Day. Nanette public speaks in court for a living; it was Nanette herself who suggested that she front the presentation and act as our main spokesperson.

Confidence simply seems to come naturally to Nanette; she has presence and people listen to her when she has something to say. This event saw Nanette effortlessly charming everyone in the press and media; easily making bizarre and arcane subject matter accessible; all of which really needed to be seen to be believed!

She wasn't nervous in the slightest at the prospect of going before the media; or about the type of questions she was likely going to get asked. After some of the court cases she had already been involved with and high court appeals she won for her company; standing before the press held no fear for her! She answered Robyn's well-meaning question "I don't think so Robyn, once they start asking us questions I sit down and I ask them to make it clear which one of us their question is directed at" Anna asked her "You feel ok Nanette?" she smiled back "Of course!"

Nanette looked beyond immaculate in her suit, with perfect make-up and hair; effortlessly très chic! It seemed like Anna came along to the Press and Media Day inspired by a famous brand of doll that once got rhymed in a song with party. Robyn and I came as we were; wearing eco-friendly clothes and a smile.

The event was to be held in the large room in which we first met The Count; the one that usually got used for weddings. Gradually the chairs filled up with members of the press and media; television cameras were set up; and right on-cue we made our entrance to sit behind a table placed on the raised platform in front of our audience.

Nanette stood up and walked around to the front "Welcome to you all and thank you so much for coming. My name is Nanette Fabienne; please allow me to introduce the people behind me. From the left to the right is Om Darke, Robyn Humphries-Darke and last but not the least Anna Kostrová (polite applause). I am one of the two team-leaders; Om Darke is the other and usual team-leader. Robyn the investigator extraordinaire the classic psychic and Anna is the expert in negative entities. The most petite person sat with Robyn is Romy Humphries-Darke; the youngest member of the team! (much laughter).

Nanette perched herself down relaxed on the front edge of the table her friends were sat behind and continued "At the personal invitation of The Count we have been staying at his castle over the last week for the in-depth paranormal investigation. We filmed all of our cases over this week's lockdown; some of you will no doubt have already viewed our channel for some of the background on who we are; so you will be aware of what we do. Our first investigation saw us looking into the mysterious case of Victorian chimney-sweep 'Bert'! Thanks to the efforts of Om Darke going beyond what we thought achievable in such the narrow time-margin, he has the film edited ready to watch; there now follows an exclusive premier of the video. Thank you and please play the film Om!"

The 'Bert' case was shown to the press and media. When it finished there was a spontaneous round of applause from the press. Nanette stood up again and once more walked around to the front "Thank you so much! Thank you all of you! Please to give a round of applause for Mr Om Darke, we really have no idea how he managed to edit this film while also looking out for us on the lockdowns. Like you, this is the first time we all see it completed, it looks superb Om; thank you so much!" The press applauded me, Nanette added "You can get some rest now Om!" (laughter). Nanette spoke again "I am sure you must have the many questions, please make it clear which one of us you are wishing to be asking something, and we do our very best to answer for you!" Nanette smiled warmly as she sat down next to me.

Alan Meredith/BBTV – Nanette, I think I speak for all us when I say you did a splendid job of work introducing your team and the film, truly professional; especially as this was not even in your first language! (the audience applauded her). I actually have two questions for you Nanette. Are you the twin sister of Mr Darke? Secondly, I hope you won't mind me saying this, we can all see you are one traffic-stoppingly beautiful woman Nanette, with your height and looks, I perhaps wrongly assume you must be a model?

Nanette - Hi Alan, thank you and thank you most kindly for making me feel happy with your applause everyone! No Alan, I don't mind you saying that, although I am blushing beetroot red under my foundation! (laughter). No, I am not the model. I do not think you would ever guess what my real day job is! (Nanette looked around the room meeting everyone in the eyes) Do you all give up? I am the lawyer specializing in commercial property planning and building contract law (shocked gasps from the audience). When not involved in a court case I am told I can be so stereotypically blonde it hurts! We all nodded in agreement with her, to much laughter from the press. Om Darke is not my brother; we are first cousins who happen to look like twins; although in reality I am five years the younger of us two.

Gill Carter/Daily Start – Mr Darke, how did you first get into being a ghost hunter?

Me – My father was also a paranormal investigator back in my native France, he is always my inspiration.

Gill Carter/Daily Start – Mr Darke, at what age did you move here to the UK and why does your father no longer investigate the paranormal?

Me – I was eleven when we moved here, somehow I lost my accent, which was certainly never intentional! My parents are helping running a commune in Italy, my father doesn't have the time now to go on paranormal investigations. He told me when I was eleven, and we moved to his native Kent, I would do more than he did with the paranormal, seems he was right.

Gill Carter/Daily Start – Mr Darke, there is an interview on your channel where you claim that if you weren't involved in the paranormal you would likely be teaching meditation or maybe martial arts; do you think you might do this in the future?

Me – Probably not now Gill. I committed to paranormal investigations from being in my late teens; in one form or another this is my vocation.

Alan Meredith/BBTV – Anna, you've got millions of followers on your channel and social media; my PA went through every single one of your posts and watched every film; you rarely share anything personal about yourselves. Please tell us all something about the woman behind the camera.

Anna – This is our plan Alan; we prefer the focus to remain on the cases. We feel our audiences tune-in to watch the cases; and are uninterested in what we ate for breakfast or what brand of phone we recommend works best out on a lockdown! (laughter) Okay, something personal about me Alan? I like peaches and I can't show you the proof as there's been nothing down there to see since I was twenty, but I honestly am a natural blonde! (loud laughter).

Philippa Lord/Woman File – Hi Anna, I like peaches too, and do feel free to show me the lack of proof later Anna! (Laughter) My blonde sadly comes courtesy of Frankie my hairdresser; I'll gladly show you the proof I'm not a genuine blonde Anna! (loud laughter) Another question Anna, what do you say to all those sceptics out there who don't believe in psychics?

Anna – I wouldn't argue or try to persuade them I am right and they are wrong. There is room for all opinions and I respect any sceptics' right to be sceptical. Are you a sceptic Philippa?

Philippa Lord/Woman File – Truthfully, I was Anna! I'd got my prepared list of questions intending to try and take you all down. I scrapped them mostly during your film, and the rest as a result of meeting you! You lot are not in any way how I expected psychics to be; you're all funny and _____ sexy; oh and I'm single Anna if you're into girls! (Laughter) Are you available for an interview later? I want to know all about you Anna and I promise to blatantly flirt! (Anna laughed; as did everyone else)

Anna – Yes Philippa, this sounds like one interview for me not to miss! (Laughter) In fact anyone wants to talk to any one or all of us when we are through here, please ask us.

Note: Anna told us that afternoon when all this was all over Philippa served as a mirror to her of how she used to be herself "I grew into being me!" was how she put where she saw herself now as a woman.

Gill Carter/Daily Start – This question is for Robyn and Anna. You said it was the first time you tried that thing you did; it was mind-blowing watching it in your film. Especially when you talked in that dialect Anna! We saw in your film you're clearly very close, you look made for one another, have you ever been a couple?

Anna – Robyn and I have such a strong understanding, I think this is obvious in the film. We never were or shall be a romantic couple Gill. We're like opposite poles of a magnet; but we have such respect and love for each another. The dialect experience was weird, I wasn't even aware of talking at that moment. I'm Czech and can't normally speak in a Scottish accent; 'Ock, I dinnie kin', see what I mean? (much laughter) If Robyn and I were ever destined to be a couple it would've happened long ago! My boyfriend and I are soon opening a community art gallery in the town outside this castle; these three cases here at the castle were my last ever paranormal investigations! We want to enjoy loving one another and raising the children we plan to have (loud applause).

Robyn – I believe Anna covered everything; we are close as friends and also professionally. I must say she smells divine to hug, and this made my task quite pleasant (laughter) Anna was the one taking the big risk, and I really do mean a massive risk! My role was simpler, to ask Anna or 'Bertie' questions and enjoy breathing in her delicious fragrance (laughter).

Anna – Thank you Robyn. I washed my hair with rose and ylang ylang shampoo especially for you knowing you would have your nose buried in it for over an hour! (hilarious laughter).

Phoebe Pascal/Ways To Wisdom – My question is for Mr Darke. How much pressure is there to always be getting the result on investigations? You still showed the video when you were drawing the blank at Yvette's place. And does every case get the video?

Me – Bonjour Phoebe! I declare before I answer this some personal interest. Phoebe is Nanette and my cousin. I am most surprised to see you here! She works for a magazine in Paris.

Phoebe Pascal/Ways To Wisdom – Yes, okay bonjour to you cousin Nanette and you cousin Om. Now please be answering my questions! (laughter).

Me – I will be answering your points one by one. There is no real pressure to get results every time, naturally there are occasions we are called in and discover nothing, or as in the case you are mentioning Phoebe, on that case the explanation was far more rational. I believe it is important to show also these films, as well as the more ghostly ones. Not every case even gets a video, over half of what we do is for people not wanting publicity, and we respect that and of course never publicly talk of these cases either.

Phoebe Pascal/Ways To Wisdom – Thanking you cousin for the answers most detailed. Please may I be asking Robyn a question? Are you the same Robyn from the Jim's Bar case? We never saw you on the film in the case.

Robyn – Guilty as charged Phoebe! I know you are asking that for the sake of everyone else here and your readers. Om and I are blissfully, and I truthfully mean blissfully, married.

Oscar Smith/Radio Ecosse – Nanette, are you staying on as part of the team when you all go home?

Nanette – No, I go back to the easier task of dealing with High Court judges and arguing down the other lawyer's case! (much laughter)

Phoebe Pascal/Ways To Wisdom – Nanette, although we have not yet seen these, you must be more than directly involved with some cases here; did you ever get scared?

Nanette – Petrified Phoebe! (laughter) Without giving away spoilers, I suggested for part of our investigation at the castle we ought to each go off solo armed with only the video camera for a lockdown; most terrifying fifty minutes of my life! (laughter) Please to keep on watching the channel and you know exactly to what I refer to when it appears on screen. I am not acting scared! (laughter)

Alan Meredith/BBTV – You people deserve to be household names; you make films looking so professional they could literally go straight to TV! I want to also ask you Mr Darke about your cousin Nanette; you know she could easily walk into a TV presenting job tomorrow? I noticed remarkably that she doesn't use scripts or even notes! Can you comment on her talent for us please?

Me – Thank you Alan. We have always enjoyed the freedom to do our own thing. We are only ever thinking of television if we still retain full creative control. From watching Nanette on camera as she went about her investigations, she was able to communicate from the very first moment with authority, she never minded taking advice, and as you point out Alan, everything she says is Nanette thinking on her feet; and in a language that is not her native tongue. She is remarkable. You are remarkable cousin!

Nanette - Mon dieu I feel quite emotional. Excuse me for crying. Give me the moment. (Nanette composes herself) Thank you Om, it means the world coming from you the kindest words you say.

Alan Meredith BBTV – You are four people with looks and charisma that's for sure; TV is your natural home! You three women could grace the cover of any magazine; you are all _____ beautiful in different ways. You are not at all how I envisaged, it's not often I see eye to eye with Philippa Lord but on this occasion I must agree with her; you three women are so _____ sexy; and you Mr Darke are like a model yourself! Can we talk later Mr Darke?

Me – Yes Alan, we can talk.

Philippa Lord/Woman File – I love you too Alan! (much laughter)

Nanette - It is two hours since we began, so unless there are any more questions, I suggest we now finish. No more questions? In that case ladies and gentlemen we thank you all for coming along. As Anna mentioned, we stay around to give any personal or group interviews for you. Thank you all once again for coming! (she received a huge round of applause)

I immediately went for an off the record conversation with Phoebe "Good to see you cousin! Thank you for coming all the way up to Scotland" she replied "Hi Om. It is good to be seeing you, Robyn and Romy; and Nanette as well" I asked "Have you called in at the farm recently?" Phoebe replied "I visit to stay there several days on my way back home. Perhaps you visit as well and we get to spend the quality time together?" I smiled "I would adore that Phoebe. And now all the people are looking at us, ask me some questions quickly cousin!" She did...

Robyn was between interviews when Philippa Lord got her woman, and began the interview with Anna. Robyn wasn't intentionally eavesdropping, but as I already said Anna has a loud voice, and so did Philippa! Robyn told me what got said later...

"Anna, can we talk now?" she answered "Yes, of course Philippa, I am all yours!" Philippa winked at her and said "If only Anna, if only!" Anna laughed. Philippa went on "Okay, I promise that I shall not go near your personal life Anna, you made it clear earlier that's off-limits. I respect you Anna and I give you my word of honour nothing personal about you will appear in my article" Anna smiled warmly and said "Thank you Philippa" she looked Anna directly in the eyes "I make no secret I want to take you back home to my bed with me right now more than anything, what can I do when you're in love? Life just sucks sometimes!" Anna of all people looked quite shocked at getting come on to; all she could respond with was "Wow!" Philippa replied "I promise not ask you directly about him Anna; did I already mention I want you in my bed?" Anna laughed as she replied "I believe you did!" Philippa then got professional, proceeding to interview Anna about how it feels to be a woman involved in psychic work, if she enjoyed her time investigating the castle; and also asked about her plans to open an art gallery. The interview lasted under half an hour. They hugged goodbye. In a stage whisper Anna said into Philippa's ear "If I wasn't spoken for you would like totally be my type; I love empowered feminine women" Philippa in an equally loud stage whisper answered back "That cute little dress of yours would look perfect on my bedroom floor!" Robyn didn't hear this next part; she saw Philippa breathing into Anna's ear whispering something. Anna breathlessly said "Philippa, it feels like we've been hugging goodbye forever, people will begin to notice us!"

Philippa looked Anna directly in the eyes as they parted "You have my number, call me babe if you ever fall out of love" Philippa kept to her word about everything she promised Anna when her article got published.

During the two hours after the official press-conference the four of us gave more interviews than we could remember. Eventually most of the press had gone, Anna, Nanette and Robyn were enjoying a glass or two of wine sitting on the bottom steps of the stairs where The Count had made his grand entrance a week earlier. Romy was with me.

"Are you okay for us to talk now Mr Darke?" this was Alan Meredith, I answered "Yes for sure Alan, are you wanting an interview or another type of conversation?" Alan smiled "I got the impression from the film are the kind of man who will cut straight through all the flim flam to the point. No Sir, it isn't really an interview I had in mind. While my colleagues were talking to you, I waited my turn and sent a few emails off to my production team" I held up my hand for him to stop "If you are going to be making any business proposals I want Robyn present; we make all decisions collectively about the direction we go in" Alan smiled wanly "Yes of course Sir, I wouldn't have it any other way!" I called across the room asking for Robyn to join me, Anna came as well and took Romy with her. Alan also called across the room "Nanette, this might interest you, would you care to join us?" She came and sat with us looking a little mystified. I said "Please continue Alan" he did "I'll just come straight out with it shall I? My producers are quite interested in signing you for a series, and possibly two" I immediately came back with "Creative control is the key Alan, we would not be taking kindly to some director telling us how to behave or what to say" Alan answered "They are fully aware of your channel and agree with me the concept works perfectly; the idea is you continue doing exactly what you do and exactly how you do it; with the only difference being your films will appear syndicated on television to many multi-millions of viewers all around the world, rather than the internet. I can't talk yet regarding fees, through syndication it would be considerably more than your earnings from the internet" I came back with "We have a loyal following on our channel Alan, I know I speak for both of us when I say we don't want to be feeling we are abandoning them" Alan laughed "Sir you for sure are one formidable person to negotiate with! How about this? One week after an episode airs globally, you can post it to your site?" Robyn asked "We film in the same way as now, with no outsiders telling us what to do?" Alan replied "Yes and yes, Robyn. No director and your husband continues on as the editor of films you record yourselves. If there is a successful recipe one doesn't go changing the seasoning or adding extra ingredients. We will gift you state-of-the-art camera technology and also a professional editing suite all as part of the deal." Robyn questioned "And we get to choose our locations?" Alan smiled at her "Yes you do Robyn" I said "Is it possible to put this all in writing, then Nanette can take a look over it for us?" Alan nodded affirmatively and said "Which brings me on to you Nanette. You have it all; you're \_\_\_\_\_ gorgeous, the camera loves you and you're naturally funny! Would you ever consider a television presenting career Nanette? Honestly you could walk straight into a job. Your sexy accent is your greatest asset after your \_\_\_\_\_ beauty"

We talked on for a little longer. Alan did put all the details we discussed into writing the same day and emailed them across that evening. We soon get back to him. We thanked him for thinking so highly of us to offer a television series and declined his offer. Alan didn't understand us when he did his pitch; we weren't tempted for a moment by possibly earning millions for selling our souls to television land; and more than that, never being able enjoy travelling anywhere again without getting recognised. Robyn and I desired to get back to simpler times above anything else.

Nanette also declined his offer; after all she had many other things to think about…

## SHOULD I STAY OR SHOULD I GO?

"Who is travelling back with Robyn and me?" This question I asked over breakfast on our last official day at the castle.

Anna said "I am staying on for a few days with the lovely photographer. He has some commitments, next week we travel together down to Kent to pick up my stuff that I still want, which actually won't be much. I'll gift mum my place in Margate. We'll call in on you to say hi!"

Nanette said "I am also staying on here for the couple of days. Peter wants to make the big official announcement about us to the press tomorrow; it seems most fitting that I ought to be present when he does this!" The other three of us looked at each other; it was Anna who finally said it "You're not, are you?" Nanette beamed at us; she got the engagement ring out of her shoulder bag, placed it on her finger and said "I am soon to be The Countess Nanette!" I confess we all cried. In a few months we went along to the wedding at the castle: it was quite exquisite; and lovely to catch-up with all of my family; after they were betrothed we couldn't wait to get away from that castle to return home!

## DONATION

Our fee arrived in our bank account a few days after we got home from our week long lockdown. This case left a sour taste for me, talking with Robyn we agreed on what to do. Normally, after our own expenses were deducted, the rest of the fee would be split between anyone else apart from ourselves who took part in the case. Nanette already made it more than clear to us she didn't want her share of the fee, obviously because of her new life and circumstances. Given our love of art galleries, this left us only one logical choice to make.

Taking out ten percent to cover our own expenses, we donated the rest of the fee to Anna and the lovely photographer to help them set up their community art gallery.

Four months on from this an email pinged into my inbox, it came from Anna; she shared that her and Countess Nanette were best-friends. She attached photographs showing their newly opened art gallery; the name on the sign above it read 'The Darke Community Art Gallery'. Anna shared other great news, she was pregnant! They got quietly married at the castle; neither of them wanted a big fussy wedding. Nanette arranged for the marriage celebrant, along with only herself and Peter to witness the marriage. We understood exactly where there were coming from; after all our marriage had been similarly intimate.

We were truly delighted for Anna and the lovely photographer; and on a personal note even more truly delighted to have missed the wedding! After visiting for Nanette's own wedding, we never wanted to see that castle ever again! Too many bad personal memories of Robyn and I ending up apart. Never again!

From now it would be only Robyn and Om Humphries-Darke loving being alongside one another on an investigation, wrapped within their indescribable love. Sounds about perfect I know; and this is exactly how it was from then on.

# 16

# WE BOUGHT THE FARM

I was born in France. I guess this isn't exactly news to you, I thought I'd mention it again anyway. More specifically I was born on my grandparent's farm in extremely rural Normandy. My mum didn't plan it this way; she shouldn't really have been surprised it happened though. My parents lived a way away in the village closest to the farm; mum was at nearly full term of her pregnancy when she insisted they visit; she went into labour that same day. There wasn't any time to get her to hospital. My grandmother delivered me in the same room my mum and her three sisters had also been born in.

I have dual nationality, I am British and French. Which do I feel the most? I identify as a father, husband, son, brother, grandson and finally a paranormal investigator; my possible nationality comes way after all of these. If you put a gun to my head and forced me to choose which side of the English Channel I fell on, firstly I would tell you that I feel at home wherever Robyn and Romy are. If you still insisted I made a choice, France would be the country. All of my extended family lives there, apart from Nanette who you already met.

Residing on the Kent Coast, we travel over to France like most Kentish folk might pop up to London. Okay, I'll be straight with you, I love France! There, I said it…

GRANDMA WISHES ROMY A HAPPY BIRTHDAY

Throughout this case I'll translate from French into English for you, of course I am not assuming that you couldn't understand if I did relate this story in French; it just seems like a sound plan, and so I am going with it.

Romy was one years old! We were celebrating the rather splendid occasion out in our admittedly smallish garden; for sure we bought our home in St Margaret's Bay for the spectacular views overlooking the white cliffs of Dover. The house was adequate for our needs when there were just the two us; the tiny outside area was becoming more of an issue as Romy grew. We didn't have any specific plans to move on to another place; but it's something Robyn and I did discuss but with no definite direction, plan or end game. We simply talked every now and again about Romy soon outgrowing the garden.

The birthday celebrations were in full swing when my phone rang; it was my grandmother wishing Romy a happy birthday! Grandma is one cool woman; a few years ago her and my grandad took on a farm manager to look after their main crops of rapeseed and lavender, and the cider orchard; grandma soon found herself able to enjoy the kind of life she couldn't have dreamt of when raising a family and looking after the farm. She took up archery of all things; she proved good as well. By and by this seventy two year old youngster entered the regional longbow finals; finishing a highly credible nineteenth out of fifty competitors, most of whom could easily be her grandchildren!

Grandad is more laid back; he loves nothing better than relaxing in his armchair reading his favourite genre of book, American cowboy stories. The man would have fitted right into the old frontier days in America, I tease him he would have had the nickname 'Snake-Eyed Jean-Luc' he pretends to scowl meanly at me playing the part; then we both laugh and hug. I am sure if grandad got the chance he would travel back to live in those times.

Back to my grandma and her call to Romy, after she was through talking to her she came back on to me "Omie I have to ask you something" both my grandparents call me Omie, it feels nice, I replied "Yes Grandma, what is it?" she hesitated "I am almost embarrassed to say, but our home feels weird. We are uncomfortable to be in there now. Maybe I get too old to make any sense Omie?" Waving at Romy who was grinning at me, I replied "We will be with you on Friday. Grandma, you are younger inside than all of us!" and after our goodbyes, we ended our call.

Later that night Robyn said "Babe, we have visited that farm a hundred times and never once felt anything paranormal; this is rather a strange one. I suppose we shall know more as we explore over the weekend"

I agreed this was weird. I booked our train tickets for Friday and when it came around, off we travelled. We took my Land Rover Defender, as we always did when knowingly heading down the rougher backroads of rural France; soon we emerged from the channel tunnel in Calais and left the train, to continue onwards to Normandy.

## OUR ODDEST AND MOST PLEASURABLE LOCKDOWN

My grandparents have a small cottage on their land; they rent this out in summer for holidays. I guess if your idea of the perfect vacation is a rural idyll, with extensive walking opportunities, this would be the place to stay.

What surprised us pulling into the farmyard is the lack my grandparent's pick-up truck anywhere to be seen; they knew when we would arrive, it was inconceivable to us they would choose not to be there to welcome us. I phoned "Grandma, we are here, where are you both?" she replied "Omie, we are in the holiday cottage, please drive only a little further and we welcome you with love in our hearts!" Okay, this got weirder by the minute. I drove down the dirt track that leads to this cottage. Their pick-up truck stood parked outside, my grandparents were both leaning on the gate of the cottage to greet us.

After our respective hello's, hugs and the huge fuss made over Romy, which she would probably quite happily have endured from then until she went off to University in nearly two decades; we got around to addressing the real reason we were there.

"Omie our farm no longer feels like home; it is making us feel uncomfortable mostly" my grandad looked sad as he explained. Robyn said "Thank you for calling us Grandad; we shall investigate for you and see if we may discover a rational reason the farm feels weird" he answered "We love you so much Robyn. You are always there for us" I said "We will do a lockdown in the farmhouse all night tonight, is it okay if Romy sleeps here with you?" they looked like I'd gifted them one million euros, a new pick-up truck and an all-expenses-paid holiday to the destination of their choice "Yes please! Romy has the best of both of you two, you do know that? She's got Robyn's most exquisite beauty and all of your presence. We are going to adore this night!" I thanked grandma for her lovely words; after the delicious vegetable soup and home baked bread that made up our evening meal, Robyn and I got ready for our oddest lockdown ever, investigating the house I was born in!

My grandparent's home always felt light and airy. Many traditional French farm properties of this period have typically small windows with low ceilings. Not so with this building; white exterior walls, large windows and high ceilings gave their home a sort of colonial feel. Robyn and I loved visiting the place; it always felt warm and welcoming. What could have so changed?

We decided to walk down to our lockdown; it was only half a mile from the cottage. On this investigation we carried no cameras or any other equipment; only the digital recorder for possible EVPs and our considerable experience of ghost hunting.

Passing through the vast vegetable patch behind the farm, we made our way around to the large white front door. We looked at one another for a moment; I put the key in the door and opened it. We paused outside, holding hands in we gingerly walked.

Our first impressions were it still felt as welcoming as ever upon entering. Robyn said "This is odd babe, I don't feel in the slightest like any spirit is anywhere in this building, how about you? Do you pick-up on anything?" I replied "No I don't babe, the place all feels exactly the same as when we visited to meet up here with Phoebe after the castle cases. We should explore every room and see from there babe".

The farmhouse was a labyrinth of rooms all on the one level. With an arm around one another, we systematically made our way from one end of the farmhouse to the other; I even opened the trap door to the attic space and we explored up there.

We gravitated towards the usual guest bedroom we stayed in when we visited. We lay on the bed for a while within our own thoughts. I finally said "You know Grandma and Grandad never did actually claim it was a ghost or anything paranormal making them feel uncomfortable in here? I think because this is what we do, them saying how they felt about living here made us think this is what they meant" Robyn answered "You are reaching the same conclusion I am, right babe? I kissed my wife "Yes Robyn. We'll think about it some more in the morning" We still had the rest of the night to spend together in the farmhouse; Romy was safe and happy; we physically expressed our deepest love for one another right through until practically the first light of dawn. We caught a couple of hours sleep, then enjoyed a shower together, after which we headed off back to the little cottage.

## THE OFFER

"Grandma you do know there are no ghosts in the farmhouse, right?" she smiled "Yes, of course Omie!" I had to ask "Why did you let us go off to do a lockdown for you?" Grandad answered this one "You seemed so determined to undergo this lockdown for us, what could we do? Did you two enjoy being all on your own in there?" he looked us each in the eyes for a moment, with a twinkle in his own eyes; we both knew exactly what the man meant, and he knew we knew! "We really did Grandad, we enjoyed it immensely!" replied Robyn, he answered "Most excellent! And now we need to talk with you and please do not feel obliged; we just talk to see what we see"

Grandma said "We cannot cope with living in the big house anymore; it is too much work for us. We used to have the daughter of our farm manager come in to help, but now she is married and gone off to live in a town far from here. We like it in our petite cottage, we are still surrounded by the land we most adore, but we easily cope with everything ourselves here" Robyn said "We thought it might be like this Grandma".

Grandad took up the story "We always thought one day to pass the farm onto one of our daughters and their family; over the last month we talk to them in a casual way to see how they feel about one day living here.

None of them are interested! Robyn and Omie, they have their lives and the farm, it is too remote for them to want to live here. I know there are thinking to sell the farm once we are gone! This is all too sad for us" there were tears in his eyes.

Robyn once more spoke "We talked Grandma and Grandad; we adore the thought of living here. We know this is really what this visit is all about; and why you invited us. This is our favourite place to be; it would be an incredible life for Romy growing up surrounded by all this space!" I took up the narrative "Here's what Robyn and I propose. We buy the farm from you at market price, what you do with the money is naturally up to you, but we thought you could split this between mum and her sisters, then they don't feel like they have lost their inheritance. Of course you will live in the cottage for many years to come and we will be right there for you if you need anything" Grandma and Grandad looked beyond pleased, he said "This is most perfect, we could not have dreamed of better! Yes to all of what you suggested; how soon can this happen?" Robyn replied "We shall put our home up for sale at a 'come and buy me' price as soon as we return. In its location it shall sell immediately of this I am sure, there are literally dozens of people waiting to move there and only so many properties come to market. Two months, maybe three at the maximum Grandad. I shall ask

Nanette to draw us up a legal contract to purchase the farm and then we are jolly well good to go!"

We bought the farm and moved to rural France.

# 17

# AUTHOR'S NOTE

Transcendental is the only way I can describe it. Writing this book became akin to some out-of-body experience. Unlike the way I usually write, THE SPIRITS AT JIM'S BAR got neither any planned plot nor any storyboarding beforehand. I commenced writing each chapter armed with only the title, to subsequently stop at some point later when the chapter seemed to have naturally reached its conclusion. Despite this abstract approach during the seven months it took to write the book, it somehow happily managed to all come together as a coherent and continuous story in the end.

The first chapter set the scene on a personal level for how I approached the writing; as much as it also set the scene for all of the action that follows. With only one section of the lockdown featured in this chapter left to write, I had on my hands all these disparate pieces of a complex puzzle laid out before me. As I wrote part three of the lockdown, set in the main bar, I was utterly astonished as I watched all these separate snippets of information came together to form a conclusion to the lockdown making perfect sense. Looking back now, until I wrote that final section, I know for sure I hadn't got the faintest idea what all those individual bites of detail actually meant. I felt like the theme to The Twilight Zone should be playing in the background to accompany me, as I finally understood the real truth behind the case; bizarrely even hidden from me until that moment!

Om Darke, the main protagonist in this novel came to me as a complete character on one cold January morning upon waking up. We leave his story here in around 2021, in what must be some parallel world that Covid has not touched or devastated. I like that Mr Darke is nothing whatsoever like me; this made him especially interesting for me to write for. I admit there is one character that appears in the book who unintentionally managed to end up quite alike my own personality; I do enjoy a little mystery and so I shall keep exactly who this might be under my hat or hood.

I do find myself pondering what happened next in the lives of Om, Robyn and Romy Humphries-Darke and even more than that, how Om Darke first started out as a paranormal investigator…

# ABOUT THE AUTHOR

In his long career Dean Fraser has variously worked as a tomato picker, antiques dealer, conceptual artist, radio presenter, and during the last twelve years has become famously known as Dean Fraser - The Quantum Poet; with ten poetry collections to his name. He adores most of all sharing his poetry with audiences. Dean considers himself primarily a storyteller, proclaiming that with his poetry he tells stories that rhyme…sometimes!

Dean contributes poetry, essays and short stories to well over a hundred magazines and e-zines around the world. THE SPIRITS AT JIM'S BAR is his first full-length novel to feature Om Darke.

www.deanfrasercentral.com

Printed in Great Britain
by Amazon